Luca clapped quietly, wanting to cheer.

Feeling happy that her son seemed to be enjoying himself.

Feeling even happier that they were here, under this shelter's protection. They were safe, at least for now.

She glanced at Mark, who stood beside her also watching the training show. He was smiling as well, and he nodded to her as if he knew what was on her mind. She appreciated his attitude.

Okay, realistically she appreciated him in many ways—although liking his looks and his sexy cowboy attitude at times even when he wasn't wearing the hat she'd seen him in before was totally inappropriate.

Well, he didn't have to know about her feelings. They were undoubtedly just an offshoot of her relief that she and her son had found a safe place to stay.

Dear Reader,

Undercover Cowboy Defender is the third in my Shelter of Secrets series, a spin-off from my K-9 Ranch Rescue series for Harlequin Romantic Suspense. As with the others in this series, it takes place at the very special Chance Animal Shelter and the nearby town of Chance, California.

In this book, a recently widowed single mother must flee her home with her young son because the person who she believes killed her husband is now after her. She is fortunately told about the Chance Animal Shelter, which protects people in trouble as well as animals. She and her son are given new identities: Luca and Nicky.

Also at the shelter are Mark Martin and his dog, Rocky, both also apparently in protection. But he is actually a K-9 cop there on an undercover assignment, and suddenly finds himself protecting Luca and Nicky, too.

I hope you enjoy *Undercover Cowboy Defender*. Please come visit me at my website, www.LindaOJohnston.com, and at my weekly blog, http://KillerHobbies.blogspot.com. And, yes, I'm on Facebook and Writerspace, too.

Linda O. Johnston

UNDERCOVER COWBOY DEFENDER

Linda O. Johnston

Recycling programs
for this product may
not exist in your area.

ISBN-13: 978-1-335-73829-5

Undercover Cowboy Defender

Copyright © 2023 by Linda O. Johnston

For questions and comments about the quality of this book,
please contact us at CustomerService@Harlequin.com.

Harlequin Enterprises ULC
22 Adelaide St. West, 41st Floor
Toronto, Ontario M5H 4E3, Canada
www.Harlequin.com

Printed in U.S.A.

Linda O. Johnston loves to write. While honing her writing skills, she worked in advertising and public relations, then became a lawyer...and enjoyed writing contracts. Linda's first published fiction appeared in *Ellery Queen's Mystery Magazine* and won a Robert L. Fish Memorial Award for Best First Mystery Short Story of the Year. Linda now spends most of her time creating memorable tales of romance, romantic suspense and mystery. Visit her on the web at www.lindaojohnston.com.

Books by Linda O. Johnston

Harlequin Romantic Suspense

The Coltons of Colorado

Shielding Colton's Witness

Shelter of Secrets

Her Undercover Refuge
Guardian K-9 on Call
Undercover Cowboy Defender

The Coltons of Mustang Valley

Colton First Responder

K-9 Ranch Rescue

Second Chance Soldier
Trained to Protect

Visit the Author Profile page at
Harlequin.com for more titles.

Like the other books in the Shelter of Secrets series, *Undercover Cowboy Defender* is dedicated to the wonderful people who devote their lives to helping other people in trouble, and also to those who work for and volunteer at shelters where dogs, cats and other animals without human families are cared for.

And, as I always do, I dedicate this book to my dear husband, Fred, as well as our dog, Cari, and our new puppy, Roxie.

Acknowledgments

Repetitious, yes, but again many thanks to my wonderful editor, Allison Lyons, and my fantastic agent, Paige Wheeler.

Chapter 1

"I want to play, Mommy." Davey stood on the wooden floor beside the chair on which Cathleen Almera sat along the outer wall of the reception room. His bottom lip was stretched in a pout, which only made him more adorable. His light brown hair was mussed up around his sweet face with its cute little nose and scowling dark brown eyes.

Cathleen wasn't surprised at his attitude. They'd been waiting for nearly fifteen minutes, and her four-year-old son liked to stay active, not sit on a chair. And so he hadn't been, mostly running around the room instead. But he now stopped momentarily.

"I understand, honey," Cathleen responded. "But right now, we have to wait until we get to see someone."

Instead of asking who or why, Davey ran from where

Cathleen was sitting, to the far end, then back toward her. Again.

Her active little son wasn't about to stay still and wait. He'd even rejected the idea of looking at cute pictures of doggies and kitties in the magazines from pet rescue organizations on a table between a couple of the chairs.

Davey was too young to understand where they were and why they were there. But it was critical not only that they wait for someone to talk to them, but also for whoever that was to accept Cathleen and her son to become residents of this place—the Chance Animal Shelter.

The animal shelter, Cathleen had learned from a friend she trusted, that was a covert location for protection of people in trouble.

Like they were.

The shelter's outside door had been unlocked and they had come inside once Cathleen had rung the doorbell, as she had been told to do. She'd also been told to just wait in the reception area until someone came to bring her in.

Cathleen hoped that Davey's activity as they waited wouldn't cause them to be rejected. She couldn't help noticing the security camera over the door across from her, which probably led into the facility.

Whether they were being watched right now, she couldn't tell, but considering the nature of this place, she had to assume they were. At least she was dressed in a nice yellow blouse and navy slacks, and had put a gray, buttoned shirt over black pants on her son. Though it was May, and they could have worn lighter clothing since it was warm in this area during the day, there was coolness at night, and though it was early now, she wanted them to be prepared to stay here.

But how long would they continue to wait?

Was this part of the decision process—determining how patient potential residents could be while waiting to be interviewed?

Observing them as they waited, analyzing what they did or didn't do?

Some other critical reason Cathleen hadn't thought of?

Maybe so. Maybe not. Cathleen didn't really know a whole lot about the place, let alone its people in charge and what they looked for. All she knew was that her friend, Mitzi Rhodes, had been in touch with the director, Scott Sherridan. Scott had told Mitzi to have Cathleen show up today to be interviewed, and to ring that doorbell when she arrived. And wait.

It helped that Mitzi was a cop in Cathleen's former hometown of Cranstone, California, and that she had been a colleague of Cathleen's now-deceased husband, George. Not to mention…

No. She didn't want to think about that whole horrible situation. Not now, although she would probably have to discuss it soon.

But Cathleen was desperate, willing to do anything to try to save Davey and herself. Despite her associations, Mitzi was a good friend and she understood Cathleen's concerns.

And this shelter sounded promising.

Yet would it be the haven they needed?

If only she knew when someone would come to talk

to her. She'd already considered going out to their car to bring in one of Davey's games so they could play, but she was afraid of missing whocver would greet them. And he wasn't interested in playing hand games with her any more than looking at magazine pictures.

No, one of the many toys and games she'd packed in the car would most likely be more appealing to him. She'd also brought a lot of clothes and other essential belongings. Things they'd hopefully be able to remove from the car and keep in whatever room was designated as theirs here at the shelter—if they were accepted.

She gathered that her vehicle would then disappear.

It belonged to Cathleen Almera, after all. If all went well, she understood from Mitzi that Cathleen and Davey Almera would cease to exist. They would be given new identities.

Mitzi had told Cathleen to tell no one any of this— that the Chance Animal Shelter helped people, too—or the few other facts about it that Mitzi had revealed. "It's a highly covert place, and very few people know what it's really about. I'm one of the lucky ones. I learned about it because of someone they took in for a short while a few months ago. I got to meet the director, Scott, virtually then, and he trusts me. Justifiably. I'm telling you only because of your…impossible situation."

Mitzi was one of the few people who knew about, and believed, that situation. Cathleen would be forever grateful to her for trying to help. And even more so if things worked out here the way she had described.

"Let's go home, Mommy." Davey stopped beside her

again. She reached out her arms to hold him, as she had several times before.

"No, sweetheart," she said. "We're going to be playing a new game soon."

She hoped. She also hoped it wouldn't be a game. And for the moment, at least, Davey stood still and hugged her back.

But when—

The door across from Cathleen suddenly opened. At last! She felt herself begin to shake, especially when a large dog, mostly black, entered. Were they in danger here?

But the dog, a Doberman she thought, was on a leash, a man right behind him.

A tall man—in a cowboy hat of all things. It looked good on him and appropriate since he was wearing a blue-and-beige-plaid shirt with rolled-up sleeves, which also seemed cowboy-like, over jeans. He appeared muscular beneath that shirt, considering the way it stretched over his chest. And he was wearing cowboy boots.

He immediately stared at her with wide blue eyes beneath thick brown brows. His wide mouth smiled. "Ms. Almera, I presume? And Davey?"

Cathleen relaxed, though just a little. Since he knew who they were, he must have something to do with this shelter. That made sense, considering where he and his dog had come from.

"That's right." Cathleen was already standing and taking a few steps in the man's direction.

Davey was suddenly beside her, hanging on to her hip while holding his hand out so the dog could sniff it. Terrified that her son would be attacked, Cathleen pulled him back and placed herself between Davey and the Doberman.

"This is Rocky," the man said, "and it's fine if Davey wants to pet him. He's a kind, loving doggy. Well trained. A good boy."

Cathleen glanced up from her son and the dog and into the man's face again. He looked sincere. Cathleen felt nervous, but the dog seemed quiet enough.

"Okay," Cathleen said. "He seems sweet." She hoped.

"I'm Mark Martin," the man said. "I'm here to meet you and learn why you're here."

Mark was actually Clark Martindale, but around here he was Mark Martin. Like everyone else, he'd been given a new identity.

And though he hopefully appeared to be one of the shelter's employees, under protection like the rest of the staff, he'd been given extra privileges, like the ability to wear his cowboy outfit now and then instead of the usual Chance Animal Shelter T-shirt.

It didn't hurt that the managers here knew he was an undercover K-9 cop. Or that they wanted him to help determine whether the shelter's security was at risk.

Or more at risk than it usually was.

He was delighted to have been given this assignment: greeting a potential newcomer to the Chance Animal Shelter and conducting this pre-interview. Mostly only managers started the process, but they were all busy now. And with his background, it wasn't surprising that the director had requested his help—which they wouldn't mention to the staffers.

"Let's sit down and talk a little, okay?" he said to the gorgeous but clearly nervous woman in front of him. He didn't know much about her—yet—except that she was hoping to be accepted here as a staff member. That meant she was in danger somehow in the outside world.

"Sure," she said, her voice shaking a little. She took her son's hand and they both headed toward the seats along the wall at the side of the room. She was maybe five foot six, judging by how she compared to his six-three. Her hair was a pretty shade of brown, arranged in waves that framed a long, smooth, attractive face with shining lips. Her clothes looked fashionable but casual; the same went for her little boy.

She sat down and Mark—yes, he made himself identify that way while he was here—took a chair a couple away from hers, with Rocky, still leashed, sitting on the tiled floor beside him. He took his Stetson off and placed it on another chair. He enjoyed wearing it but didn't always feel it appropriate here in the shelter.

For an initial interview though? Why not?

He wasn't surprised when Davey didn't sit. Mark, along with Director Scott Sherridan, had watched the two of them for a short while on the security feed in the shelter's office. They'd both commented on the child's energy.

Mark thought it was cute but wondered if Scott would reject these two because of what the boy might be like within the shelter. Would he require additional supervision? Would he be difficult to deal with when some of the shelter animals were nearby?

Mark would actually like to see what could be done with a kid like that, but it was entirely up to Scott.

Fortunately, the guy in charge had also seemed amused, despite voicing some concern. He'd told Mark to go talk with the mother and let him know how it went.

Although, Mark knew Scott would also be watching that discussion via the cameras in the reception area. He hoped he asked the right questions, which was likely since he'd already been told what to address.

He also hoped he got the right answers.

Time to find out.

"Okay," he said to Cathleen, who leaned toward him a bit, staring him straight in the face, her hazel eyes blinking as she bit her lower lip. "Just so you know, once you and I are done here, you'll be interviewed in more detail by the director, but I can get you started. What do you know about the Chance Animal Shelter?"

She moved back. "Is that a trick question? It's a very special animal shelter, right? And—well, if I tell you what I understand, it'll be clear I've been told things I'm probably not supposed to know, so you'll reject me. Or keep me captive so I don't tell anyone else. Which one?"

He laughed, but before he could answer Davey came up to them. "Mommy, can I see those pictures now?"

Cathleen glanced at Mark then nodded at the boy. "Good idea. That way you can settle down a bit. But you'll need to look at them yourself because Mommy's busy." She rose and led her child to another chair, one near a small table that held a few magazines, and he sat. She handed Davey a couple, opening one until she found pictures of some rescue dogs and cats, and placed them on his lap. Then she returned to her chair. "He must be getting tired," she said softly. "Maybe that's a good thing. It'll give us a chance to talk."

"Definitely a good thing. And as far as what you know about the shelter? Scott said he was contacted about you by someone he trusts, so you can tell me the truth."

She nodded. "Okay. I trust Mitzi too." She looked down at her hands, which she held in her lap.

Her fingers were slender and her nails were short, covered in pale pink polish. Pretty hands.

Pretty woman.

But that was irrelevant.

Her need, her reason for coming here? That was what Mark had to find out.

"So…" she began, looking up to stare him in the face. "I understand this is a wonderful shelter for taking in needy pets and finding them new forever homes."

"That's right. Anything else?" Mark prompted.

She nodded. Her eyes focused on his as her chin rose. "And it's also a wonderful shelter for taking in needy people and giving them a home. But though they appear to the world to be homeless people who are brought in to help care for the animals, they…they are needy in other ways. In danger. And they're given new identities and eventually found new lives in places different from where they're originally from."

She stared at him now almost defiantly, as if expecting him to reject what she'd said, to deny it, possibly to protect this place.

But what she'd said was exactly right.

Mark knew he had to be careful though. Not that he expected this woman, here with her child, to be attempting to dig out the truth and trumpet it to the world. Still, he hadn't learned what he needed to so Scott would allow her to stay.

"Okay, then. I assume you want to be taken in here, the way you described. So tell me what danger you're in." He leaned forward and stared into those pretty eyes. She then looked away.

But she immediately turned back to him, her expression somewhat defiant.

"Okay," she said. "But I don't want Davey to hear."

"Fine. Let's go across the room and talk."

They did. They stood near the security camera, a good thing because Scott should be able to hear them. They both faced Davey, who continued to look through the magazine, seeming awed by the pictures—also a good thing as his mother started to talk.

"Here's the situation. I— My husband George was a police officer in our hometown of Cranstone, California. It's near Sacramento. He…he recently lost his life while on duty." Her voice had been low before as she'd glanced toward Davey, but now Mark had to move closer to her to hear, hoping Scott was able to hear too. "It was during an attempted arrest. The suspect…shot him." Tears filled her eyes as she continued to watch her son.

"I'm so sorry," Mark said, also keeping his voice

low. Was that suspect now after her? Was that the danger she was fleeing? He waited, though, to hear what she would say next.

"Thank you." She hesitated, then said, "His fellow officers seemed so sympathetic. So kind. Only…" She paused.

Ah. Maybe this was where the danger came from. "Only?" he prompted.

"One of them, Morley Boyle, seemed to try hard at first to help us. But he wouldn't leave us alone." She was breathing hard now, not looking toward either Mark or her son but at the floor. "Wouldn't leave me alone. It was as if… Well, he wanted to step in where George had been. Only, George and I— That's not relevant. But that cop tried to seduce me. And when I complained to his supervisor, he convinced the superior officers that I was so stressed I was making things up. But I wasn't. And he threatened me. And Davey. A lot. And…well, he kept doing it. I even began to wonder if he'd been the one who killed George, and mentioned that to the cops, but I'm not sure they took it serious."

Interesting, Mark thought but remained quiet.

"I finally told the officer who sent me here—Officer Mitzi Rhodes, who'd been a good friend of mine before that. I don't know if she accepted that Morley could be a murderer, but she apparently did believe he was threatening me. She's the one who contacted Scott Sherridan, who she told me was in charge here. And, so, here I am." She took a deep breath. "Davey and I had to get out of there, and this sounded like the ideal situation for now. Can we stay?"

Mark wanted to shout yes, but it wasn't up to him. He wanted to hear more.

He wanted to know more about that rat of a cop Morley so he—a K-9 cop himself—could go after him. But all he could say for now was, "We'll see. I'm one of the staff members here. I was sent to do your preliminary interview. We staff members are also under the shelter's protection."

She looked baffled. "You're a staff member, in danger? What happened to you?"

I'm lying, he thought. "If you get to stay, I'll tell you. But right now, I need to tell your story to our director and let him decide whether to interview you to determine if you can stay."

"What will you say to him?" Her voice was shrill now and her eyes had grown teary once more. "Will you please, please recommend our being able to stay?"

Before Mark could state a resounding yes, the door he had walked through earlier opened.

Scott Sherridan walked in.

He was tall and wore jeans with a denim work shirt with a red-and-brown Chance Animal Shelter logo on its pocket. The logo was the outline of a dog.

The director was smiling grimly.

"You talked to Mark first because I asked him to find out some things about you, as he indicated. I'm Scott Sherridan, Ms. Almera. I'm the director here, and I've been listening by way of the speakers on the security camera. I still have some questions, so we'll go talk. But considering what you told Mark, I suspect you'll soon be able to consider yourself a staff member here at the

Chance Animal Shelter. If so, Davey will be welcome here too. For now, let's go inside, and you and I will talk. Davey can stay with us, too, of course. Are you ready?"

"Of course," she said. She nevertheless aimed a quick glance in Mark's direction. She surely wasn't looking for his okay, was she?

Or was she hoping that he, too, would stay with them as Scott asked his questions?

Well, he wouldn't be there.

But he would be thinking the whole time, maybe longer, about what they were saying…and wondering how it went.

Chapter 2

Cathleen walked over to where Davey stood near the back of the room now, petting Rocky on the head. He'd started doing that during the minute Cathleen met Scott, but she'd been watching and noted that Mark was too. And smiling. He obviously trusted his dog, and apparently rightfully so. Rocky snuggled his face against Davey's hand, very friendly despite being a breed of dog Cathleen had heard could be aggressive.

"Let's go, honey," she told her son, holding out her hand.

He moved his from the dog and grabbed Cathleen's hand as he looked up at her, eyes wide as he smiled. "Are we going home?"

"No," she said, attempting to sound happy and perky. "We're going to visit more of this fun place. I'm hoping we'll get to see some more doggies." Was she exaggerating? This was ostensibly an animal shelter, after all.

"That's right," Scott told her with a nod. "We're going to go through that door there." He gestured toward the inside door. "We'll go into another room soon, but first we'll head to the end of the hall where some really great dogs are hanging out."

Cathleen felt relieved. And interested. She liked dogs a lot, so if they did wind up staying, she'd be delighted to help take care of the rescue pups. She would learn the ways the people in charge—like Scott—wanted them cared for, and she'd help teach Davey too.

Being here would be very different from the job she'd recently quit as an accountant for the CPA firm she'd been with for seven years.

"Great," she said. She watched with interest as Mark preceded them to the door and used a key card to open it.

A good thing, she figured, for an apparently protective place like this, even though the front door into the reception area had been open.

Mark put his cowboy hat on and stepped back, Rocky leashed at his side. He gestured for Cathleen and Davey to go through first. She figured that was fine but glanced at Scott anyway. He nodded, smiled and gestured too.

As she and her son entered the long beige hallway, Cathleen noticed that the first door on the left, which was closed, had a large sign that identified it as a veterinary clinic.

What a good idea, she thought. The animals here would not only have attention but good medical care.

She was also delighted to see, beyond a few more closed doors, there were small enclosures containing dogs. Not many, but she anticipated they'd see a lot more if they were permitted to stay. Some of these dogs were small, toy-size, and others were medium, including a cocker spaniel mix. All appeared excited to see people.

"Oh, Mommy! Doggies!" Clearly, Davey was excited. "Can I play with them?"

"Sorry, sweetie. Not now. But maybe we'll get to meet some later." Cathleen watched her son without looking at either Scott or Mark. She figured her hopes were clear but attempting to beg with her expression didn't seem like a good idea.

Scott stopped at one of the closed doors beyond the vet clinic. "Why don't we go in here?" he said to Cathleen. It wasn't really a question. "And please join us with Rocky, Mark."

Cathleen immediately led her son inside. Interesting. Mark was apparently going to participate in this interview. Of course, she'd already informed him about the gist of the problem that had led her here.

The space looked like a small meeting room with several chairs inside. Just like with the rest of the building she had seen so far, the floor was tiled and the plastered walls off-white. "Please sit down," Scott said.

Cathleen did, and was glad when Mark put his hand out to lead Davey into a corner with Rocky. He started to play a few games with his dog and the boy, including rolling a ball that Rocky chased, so Davey was fortunately distracted from what was being said.

Yet she was certain Mark was listening.

For the next twenty minutes, she felt like she was on trial.

What she said to Scott, as softly as she could, was the same as what she'd told Mark, but with more detail.

She again related that her husband George had been a Cranstone police officer. During an attempted arrest, the suspect had shot and killed him.

"I-it was horrible," Cathleen said hoarsely. "We'd been having some issues, but we'd ultimately decided to stay together." Maybe that was too much information. Or not. She aimed a glance at her son, tears filling her eyes yet again. He was young enough that he hopefully wouldn't understand all of what she was saying—if he even paid attention to it, which he fortunately wasn't doing.

"I'm sorry," Scott said, then, "Please continue."

"Everyone on the force seemed so sympathetic, including George's partner, Officer Morley Boyle. He'd been George's friend. Mine, too, somewhat. Plus, he seemed highly concerned and protective of Davey and me, which I appreciated—at first."

She grew quiet. It was hard to go on. It was hard to even think about it.

But Mark looked up from where he played with Davey and tilted his head toward her, as if encouraging her to continue. And so she did, even more quietly. She didn't think Davey was listening, fortunately. He seemed much too engaged in his play with the Doberman and ball.

Still…

Very softly, she described how Morley had tried unsuccessfully to seduce her—more than once. He'd seemed sure she would be interested, especially since George had told his partner that Cathleen had asked for a divorce but they'd decided to work through it. But then George was suddenly gone from her life. Morley had said he wanted her to be happy—and that the two of them could have a relationship.

"My rebuffing didn't stop him. He even began stalking, threatening to hurt..." She looked at Davey, trying hard not to break down. She lowered her voice even more, and Scott leaned closer to her. "If...if I didn't become his lover. And when I reported him, he convinced his superior officers and others that I was so stressed I was making things up."

"I see." Scott was nodding, his expression grim. "And I gathered from what I heard you tell Mark before that you now wonder if he, and not the incarcerated suspect, was the one who killed George, right?"

She nodded, saying nothing.

"I assume, since you're here, that Morley has continued to come after you and claim his own innocence to his superiors."

Her nod grew stronger. She attempted to make herself smile, which wasn't easy. "I don't think the department bought my argument, but even if the police do consider him a suspect, what suspect doesn't proclaim his innocence?"

Scott's brief laugh came out as a snort of sorts that allowed Cathleen to actually smile—for an instant.

"Anyway," she continued, "I fortunately told my friend Mitzi what was going on and she believed me. She's the one who contacted you."

Scott nodded. "Yes, I know Mitzi. She was very concerned about you. She didn't tell me much, though, and now I can understand her concern."

Good, Cathleen thought. But was it enough?

Would Davey and she be permitted to stay at the Chance Animal Shelter, for their safety?

Of course, all she knew about the place was what Mitzi had told her. Looking it up online, all she could find was that it was a respected pet shelter that also took in some homeless people to help care for the resident animals.

There'd been nothing mentioned about how those alleged homeless were given new identities to protect them from the dangers in their real lives.

That info had come from her friend, which had certainly prompted Cathleen to bring her son here in the hope they could escape the horrible situation George's former partner had put them in.

If they weren't accepted? Well, Cathleen had considered a lot of alternatives, including returning to Cranstone, which would be potentially the worst of them.

Another option: head back to Phoenix, where she'd grown up. Her parents were still there. Except the way Morley had been acting, she was afraid that might not be enough. That she and Davey wouldn't escape the danger and would end up putting her family in danger as well.

Her brother was in Minneapolis, but he had a wife and kids and...well, no sense endangering them either.

The most important thing was to keep Davey safe. And herself, too, as much as possible. Of all the possibilities she had considered, none seemed like a good, safe choice.

Except, potentially, this place—assuming it was the kind of place Mitzi had described to her.

"You're awfully quiet," Scott said, interrupting her reverie. "Anything you want to ask?"

"Lots," she said. "But the main thing is, is this as protective a place as Mitzi suggested?"

"I know Mitzi told you some things about this place, which is fine, although we attempt to keep what we're about as secret as possible. But she's right. We do protect some people as well as the animals we take in."

"She didn't tell me much," Cathleen admitted, "but what she said sounded...well, highly appealing under my circumstances. And now, I'd like to ask..." She hesitated, looking the shelter's director sitting beside her straight in his penetrating blue eyes.

"If you and Davey can stay here?" Scott glanced down at her son on the floor then back up at Cathleen. "Thanks to Mitzi, we've done a little checking into your situation and, at least for now, the answer is yes."

Tears rose again to Cathleen's eyes as she reached out, taking Scott's hand. "Oh, thank you. Thank you. I promise I'll do everything I can to help out here at the shelter."

"Taking care of your son should be a major factor. He'll be the first child we've brought in here. And both of you can help care for the animals we shelter."

"Absolutely," Cathleen said, standing and reaching out for her son.

"Right now, let's go to my office and we'll work out some of the details—including who you'll be from now on."

* * *

Mark listened to the conversation as much as he'd been able to during his enjoyable game of rolling the ball with the little boy, Rocky sometimes going after the ball and placing it back down on the ground near one or the other of the humans.

He'd appreciated hearing Cathleen's story with the additional details she'd given Scott. Although he could understand why a guy other than her husband might have hoped to seduce a woman as attractive as she was, the circumstances she'd described were horrendous. He'd already had an urge to jump in and help her by dealing with the man who'd treated her terribly—and might even have murdered her husband—so it was a good thing he was here on an important assignment. Otherwise he might take off for Cranstone and do more than arrest the guy.

And that wouldn't necessarily be good for anyone.

For now he would do as he was supposed to: hang around and attempt to learn if one of this shelter's most important features, its secrecy, was currently at risk from the inside.

Scott and his managers had recently received hints of security breaches within the shelter. The source? Some local Chance cops who wouldn't reveal their sources—at least not yet. Not even to Scott, who was himself a member of that same police force.

"Mommy!" his little playmate shouted as Cathleen stood when Scott did and came over to him.

"We're going inside this fun place," she told him.

"We'll probably get to see more dogs. Kitties, too, I think. But not right away."

No, from what Mark gathered, they'd be heading to Scott's office to go over paperwork.

And to start the change of identities for these new residents—who would become staff members, which was what the official residents were called.

Mark wondered what Cathleen's and Davey's new names would be. He would find out soon.

And, like him, they'd be given new backgrounds as well. He didn't change that he was originally from Texas, at least. No, he was even able to wear his Stetson and other appropriate clothes sometimes around here, despite the fact he was supposed to look like a staffer.

Since he was a K-9 cop with the Chance Police Department, people who worked with him there were used to seeing him in uniform. Most people seeing him out of uniform wouldn't think he was a K-9 cop though, partly since Dobermans like Rocky were seldom chosen as police dogs these days because of their reputation as being aggressive and not always obedient. But not Rocky, who was mostly sweet, but well trained enough to be one great K-9 when given commands.

"Hey," he said. "I'll come along with you for now." Inside the shelter, though not to Scott's office.

"Can we play again?" Davey asked, looking up at Mark from where he held his mom's hand as they went through the door.

"Sometime," he said, "though not right away."

"But I like to play with you."

That made Mark smile. A lot. "I like to play with you

too." He looked at Cathleen's face and nodded. "Your son's quite a fun ball player," he said.

He genuinely hoped he'd have more opportunity to play with the kid. He liked kids. Maybe wanted some of his own someday. But that meant having a solid relationship with the right woman, and he hadn't met her yet.

Or had he—in the woman he was now looking at?

No way. He'd just met her. She had safety issues and was about to become a real staff member here. He might need to help protect her, but the fact that she was so beautiful and sweet and needy…? Irrelevant.

"I… Thank you for playing with him," Cathleen said. "It helped distract him from…from things he shouldn't have heard, even though he was unlikely to understand much of it."

They were back in the hall now, standing just outside the fences of the dog enclosures. Davey seemed enraptured again.

Scott was standing at the door at the end of the hall, glaring slightly at them.

"I think you'd better catch up with our director," Mark said. "You've got things to do."

"We'll see you again, won't we?" Cathleen asked. "I mean, I know Davey will want to play with you."

Was there another reason she wanted to see him again?

He shouldn't hope so, but he did. "I'll be around," he said. "Glad to play games with your son. And maybe we can play some games, too, one of these days."

He didn't stop to explain what kinds of games he might mean but continued down the hall, Rocky leashed at his side, until Scott used a card to unlock the door and led them into the shelter area.

Games. Cathleen had the impression Mark was alluding to…well, something other than playing ball on the floor with his dog and her son.

If she didn't have something important to do now, she would have followed to ask what he'd meant.

There was something about that guy in the cowboy hat and boots that she liked—and not only because he was so sweet to her son, although that was definitely a factor.

Cathleen had never thought she'd be attracted to a cowboy sort. She'd grown up in Arizona, lived there till she'd moved to California, never really got into watching Westerns on TV or movies, yet—

"This way," Scott said. After exiting the entry building, they went outside into an area that seemed amazing, confined, and yet vast and inviting.

There was a walkway close to them between two concrete buildings that each appeared several stories high. Beyond, there was a long, grassy lawn surrounded on the sides by a rectangular concrete walkway with several buildings around it. Was that where the animals were kept? Cathleen imagined so.

But for now, Scott, holding Davey's hand, pointed to the concrete building on the left. "Our cafeteria is downstairs. There are apartments upstairs."

As Mark went into the courtyard beyond them, Scott told her that there were offices in the building to the right, as he led her in that direction. They followed

Scott up the wooden stairs after he released Davey's hand, Cathleen holding a rail on one side and encouraging Davey to do so on the other, to the extent he could reach it, which mostly wasn't the case. But he did touch the wall at the side of the stairway and continued to hold her hand.

At the top, there was a platform with a door at the rear. "Our offices are in here." He led them inside.

There was a hallway with several doors, presumably offices of the shelter's managers, Cathleen figured. Scott led them to the far end, where he used a card to open the last door.

He gestured for Cathleen to enter, and she and Davey did so.

The office was nice enough, with a large metal desk, a computer on top and comfortable-looking chair behind it, and several chairs facing it. A placard on the wall behind the desk showed the same logo as on Scott's shirt, designating the Chance Animal Shelter.

Cathleen helped Davey onto a chair and sat on the one beside it, hoping her son wouldn't go on one of his running sprees.

Apparently having a similar concern, Scott reached inside a drawer in his desk and pulled out a pad of paper and a pen. "You know what, Davey?" he said. "I'd love for you to draw me pictures of doggies." He glanced at Cathleen as if asking her whether that was possible.

She doubted whatever her son drew would look much like a dog, but at least that gave him a purpose. "Great idea," she said.

After watching to make sure Davey was occupied

for the moment, Cathleen looked at Scott, who took a file folder from the desk, removed some paperwork, and handed it to her. It was an official-looking contract, with several pages of rules and regulations attached. "This is our agreement you'll need to sign to be able to stay here."

She swallowed as she accepted the contract and read through it as quickly as she could, knowing she would need to go through it more thoroughly later. She would be agreeing to have her identity changed and to live here in accordance with the rules provided to her. Most importantly, she would keep the place secret.

That all worked for her, so she took the pen he handed to her and signed.

"You'll need to look through those later, in more detail," Scott acknowledged. "They're essentially the rules governing living here at the shelter, as well as information about the place and its purpose. Be sure to let me know later if anything seems to be a problem."

And she and Davey would then be kicked out, she figured, at least depending on the severity of her concern.

No, for now she would have to live with whatever she read, whatever she saw. And if anything turned out to be a problem, at least she would be far away from the worst of her problems, Morley. She'd have to figure out then what to do, but she'd just have to see…

"Now, here comes the part that I know you were informed about at least somewhat by Mark. Our staff members—that's what we call our residents—live here at least temporarily, and they're all provided with new identities. That means new names, which we have to choose so we can use them appropriately in the future while helping to take care of you."

Protect us, Cathleen understood.

Like Mark. The idea of him helping to take care of her—no. She might be curious about his background, but he was also a staff member, here under protection. Hopefully they would become friends. She'd had enough of men and relationships.

"Got it," she said. "So—" She glanced at her son, who was in fact drawing what might be dog faces on the paper. At least there were round things that resembled eyes, and shaggy things that could be animal ears. She felt a pang of pride. But then she looked back up at Scott. "So, who are we?"

"I'm very glad to meet you, Luca," he said, smiling at her. Then he looked down at her son. "And I'm also delighted to meet Nicky." He reached into a drawer, then handed her logo-imprinted T-shirts, a light blue one that looked her size and an orange one that looked like her son's. "Welcome to the Chance Animal Shelter."

Chapter 3

Mark watched as Scott took Cathleen, with Davey, into the office building. He was aware of what would happen there: signing of the paperwork, followed by Scott accepting Cathleen and her son here as staff members and giving them new identities. At least, that was what should happen if all went well.

He'd gone quickly upstairs in the other building to leave his hat and boots in his apartment and change into his T-shirt, jeans and athletic shoes. Yes, most of the folks around here had occasionally seen him in his treasured cowboy regalia, but he was about to work like a staff member, so he needed to look like one too.

He headed for the central area of the shelter, deciding which building to enter with Rocky. It was late morning now on this mid-May day, too early for lunch. He continued to the far end, figuring that was where he would see some of the staff members walking dogs, or working on training, as they usually did around now.

Sure enough, he and Rocky soon caught up with Chessie, who was pacing Spike toward the furthest part of the paved walkway, past the buildings where different-sized dogs were housed and near the building that held cats and the few other kinds of sheltered pets. Mark had only been here for about a week so he didn't know anyone well. But he'd met most of the staffers as well as the animals and had been given a rundown on some of their backgrounds—both rescued pets and people.

Chessie wore a Chance Animal Shelter T-shirt. Hers was blue and long-sleeved despite the likelihood that the day would become warmer as it grew later. His was beige and short-sleeved.

"Hi, Chessie," he said as he and Rocky joined her. She was a nice-looking young woman, with light hair, green eyes and a hopeful expression. He knew she had recently gotten herself into trouble; there'd been some difficulties with a few visitors to the shelter who had been involved in a really bad situation—a murder, in fact. She'd apparently been too kind to the visitors, definitely forbidden.

He also knew she had become a shelter staff member because of her husband's multiple attempts to kill her. And though she hadn't been completely forgiven for what she'd done, management hadn't found a situation outside where she'd be protected enough, even with her current new identity, so here she still was.

Leashed at her side was a German shepherd, a retired K-9 that, Mark had been told, was now also a shelter resident and would continue to be. Spike helped to protect residents, thanks to his background, and he was apparently one of the favorite dogs around here. Mark could understand why.

At the moment, Rocky and Spike traded nose sniffs. Apparently, the Doberman liked this resident too.

"Hi, Mark." Chessie smiled at him a little shyly. Was she flirting? If so, he wouldn't encourage it. He needed to be friendly with the residents and to learn what he could from them. He even liked some more than others. But moderate, protective friendship was all there could be.

His mind moved until he pictured lovely, worried Cathleen…and he brought it back to reality. Quickly.

Caring for her any more than anyone else around the shelter just wasn't going to happen.

"So," he said, "what are you and Spike doing out here? Are you teaching him anything? Or is he teaching you?"

"Probably the latter," said a voice from behind him. He turned to see another staff member, Leonard, also with a dog. They must have come from the closest building since the dog with him was one of the larger ones—Jade, who was a dark brown Great Dane mix.

Mark had seen Leonard around the shelter before but hadn't had many chances to talk with him. He was curious why a guy so young had been taken in. Because of his age, he'd been put near the top of Mark's suspect list, but that was ridiculous. Age didn't matter. Personality issues did. Mark vowed to keep an open mind about the kid, especially since, when he'd had a brief discussion with Scott about Leonard, he'd learned that the director trusted him, though he hadn't revealed why Leonard was there.

"Have you worked with Spike before?" Mark asked Leonard as Chessie and Leonard traded leashes. He figured the answer was yes. He had the impression that all staff members were encouraged to get to know the former K-9 and learn from him even more than they'd be able to teach the old dog new tricks.

How would little Davey do with him? Or his mother?

"Yep." Leonard turned to his companion dog, bringing Mark's mind back to the present, and said, "Spike, sit."

That, he did, unsurprisingly, moving away from Rocky, who also sat. Both dogs took spots on the grass on one side of the concrete walkway, which was probably more comfortable.

"Good boy," Mark said, not surprised that Chessie said the same thing to Jade, patting him gently on the head.

"I can show you more," Leonard said. "Or do you already know how to train dogs? Or work with those that are already trained?"

Mark forced himself not to grin or to say anything that would allow Leonard to ferret out his background as a K-9 cop. "I don't know much, but Rocky and I have been learning a lot from each other. And I'll be very happy to watch you train Spike or any other dog around here. You and Jade, too, Chessie."

"I've been doing it here for a while," she said. "I'd be

glad to give you a demonstration. I think any of us would like to do that. I know you've seen some in the short time you've been here but around here that's one of the most important things. Spike won't be adopted out, but I've seen quite a few dogs go, and some cats too. The dogs always need to have some training before people are willing to adopt. That's what we're taught here. And... well, though I've seen some dogs get adopted, I don't get to meet their new people or anything."

"That makes sense," Mark said. "I hope a lot of the dogs I meet here also get adopted, although not Rocky. He's mine."

"How were you allowed to bring your own dog here?" Leonard asked.

Mark noticed a couple more staffers had exited nearby buildings with dogs. More training would occur, he figured, which meant good attention for these dogs.

"Long story that I'm not supposed to talk about." Mark guessed that everyone here would understand that no one could be forced to talk to other staff members about their background or what had brought them to the shelter. That was part of what this covert place was about.

"Got it," Leonard said.

Mark noticed one of the managers, Telma, heading their way from the office building.

"Hi, all of you," she said when she reached them. "And Spike, Jade and Rocky too." Mark figured she was in her thirties. She wore her usual bright green Chance Animal Shelter T-shirt and jeans. She moved to pat each dog on the head and then turned back toward Mark. "Hey,

Mark," she said. "Scott asked me to come get you. He'd like to talk to you in his office now, if that works for you."

No question about whether that would work for Mark. Anyone here would immediately follow Scott's instructions.

He wondered what it was about. Something to do with Cathleen? The director had most likely just interviewed her about staying here, as had Mark. Did Scott want Mark's gut instincts about whether Cathleen and her kid should stay here?

Was it something else altogether, and nothing to do with Cathleen?

He would soon find out.

"Yeah, it works for me," he told Telma.

"Sounds good." She immediately took over chatting with Leonard and Chessie while patting the dogs in their care.

Mark and Rocky headed back down the paved pathway toward the office building across from the cafeteria and apartments. He wished he'd had the opportunity to visit some dogs in the buildings along the way, but he'd done the right thing talking with the staffers.

He should be able to visit some of the dogs later, as well as have conversations with additional staff members.

Mark had been in Scott's office quite a few times since joining the Chance Animal Shelter group. Usually, after visiting Scott, he'd tell anyone who asked that his problems at home were still rampant and that the director advised him a lot.

The reality was that Scott and he talked about anything Mark might have learned through his interactions with staffers. Anything that indicated any one of them was somehow leaking secrets to people outside the shelter, such as where they were and why, and what this place was really about.

So far, Mark had only been able to advise Scott about suspicions resulting from his intuition. He had no proof any staff member was doing anything inappropriate with the outside world.

So what did Scott want to talk to him about now?

He knew he'd find out in a minute. He was about to enter the office building with Rocky when he saw Cathleen and Davey enter the building facing it with Nella Bresdall, another manager who also happened to be Scott's girlfriend. Close girlfriend. As far as Mark could tell, they lived together in their home off the Chance Animal Shelter campus, someplace downtown, although he hadn't seen them there when he'd sneaked away from the shelter to go to the Chance police station where he worked as a cop, which he did fairly often—mostly during the daytime. From what he understood, they both also had apartments here where they stayed sometimes, separately. But both left the shelter most nights, leaving other managers in charge.

Where was Nella taking Cathleen and her son? Was she going to introduce them to their new apartment here at the shelter? That would make sense.

But so would a visit to the cafeteria. It was nearing lunchtime, but even if it wasn't close to an official mealtime, a little guy like Davey might want a snack.

Well, it was unlikely Mark would find out. They'd

slipped inside the building too fast for him to even wave. A gesture that would have been appropriate from any guy they'd met here. He wouldn't have worried about appearing to be too interested in the lovely woman who piqued his interest.

He quickly entered the office building and hurried up the center stairway with Rocky. They went through the door on the top floor, into the hallway, where they walked to the end. Mark knocked on Scott's door.

It opened within a few seconds and the director stood there. "Great. You're here. Come on in. I have an assignment for you, one I think will be fun but also important." He gestured for Mark and Rocky to follow him into the office before Mark could ask any questions.

Mark sat on a chair facing the desk, Rocky lying on the floor beside him like the good dog he was.

"So what's my assignment?" Mark kept his tone light. It didn't sound as if Scott was about to have him start following one of the staffers, interviewing or keeping that person under close surveillance—all Mark had assumed would be part of what he would be doing to help ensure the people living here weren't doing anything to harm the vital shelter. So far, he'd mostly been getting to know people and pets, and telling Scott what he'd been up to.

"I want you first to help Cathleen bring their belongings in from their car, which is parked outside. And then I want you and Rocky to give Cathleen and Davey a tour of the whole shelter, introduce them to whoever you see, both staffers and animals. Then it'll be lunchtime and you can accompany them to the cafeteria. They're newbies and don't know anyone, let alone the location. Oh, and so you know, from now on Cathleen is Luca, and Davey is Nicky."

"So you've accepted them here? That's great—or at least I'd hoped it would be. They seemed legitimate to me when I talked to Cath—er, Luca—but what do I know?"

"A lot, and you're learning more." Scott smiled and stood. "And for now, since you've already met them, I want you to keep your ears open to ensure she really is as legit as she seems and not just here to get more info about the place. Although, if I thought that was the case, I would not have accepted them, of course, but they're our first new staffers since those latest rumors began."

"Got it," Mark said. That was why he was there, after all.

"Nella is showing them to the apartment they'll be living in, in the building. Fourth floor, unit R. You can meet up with them there. Okay?"

"Sounds good to me, boss." Mark stood, too, and so did Rocky. Thanks to his initial impression of the woman and her son, Mark doubted she was the kind of person he was there to find, assuming that kind of person was there at all—and he'd found no evidence so far. "I'll let you know how it goes."

Luca—yes, she made herself start thinking about who she was, using her new name—was thrilled!

She stood near the door of their new apartment, still scanning its entry and living room while Nella stood with Davey—no, Nicky, now—near the window, pointing out things in the courtyard below. She and her son had already changed into their new shirts.

They had taken an elevator up here. Luca had seen a stairway downstairs just outside the door to the cafeteria, but Nella had told her she'd be on the fourth floor and suggested they ride up there rather than walk. Luca had agreed. Maybe someday she would walk it with Nicky, but not today.

Their unit was near the end of the hallway, and they passed several doors getting to it. Nella had opened the door with a key card that she'd then handed to Luca.

The door opened onto the attractive wooden floor that spread into the living room. The place was furnished, and although there was nothing elegant about the fluffy gray sofa and matching armchair, or the short coffee table between them, it looked homey.

The living room opened into a kitchen, and a small hall that had two bedrooms opening onto it, so her son could even have his own room. The bathroom's door was between the bedrooms.

Nice. Very nice.

Sure, the apartment here was only a fraction of the size of the home they'd left in Cranstone. But there, she'd been terrified every day that Morley wouldn't just call her, or even ring the doorbell now and then and demand that she let him in, but would burst inside and do whatever he wanted to her.

In front of her son.

And maybe hurt Davey—no, Nicky, now—too.

Here, her enemy didn't know where she was. Would hopefully never find out. And if he somehow did, there was no way he could simply come inside and hurt them. Not with all the barriers keeping unwanted visitors out of the Chance Animal Shelter. Physical barriers.

Barriers of caring, protective people too.

Like the man she'd first met. Mark.

Luca liked this apartment. She was amused at how interested Nicky seemed in what Nella was pointing out.

Was it appropriate for them to go walk around outside, maybe even visit the shelter animals? Hopefully so. They were now residents, after all. She was a shelter staff member, the way she understood it. She was supposed to help take care of the resident pets, and that meant Nicky surely could help her too. But she had to learn more about them.

For now, she would just ask Nella if it was okay for her to wander inside the shelter area with her son.

She walked to the window, and Nella turned to look at her, aiming the smile already on her face in Luca's direction. "Nicky has lots of questions about this place," she said.

"I'm not surprised," Luca replied. "Can he and I go downstairs and look around?"

"Sure, but just a minute. I've got some stuff to do to get ready for lunch, but Scott told me that you're about to get a guide to give you a quick tour before you head back to this building to eat." She pulled a phone from her pocket and pressed a number. "We're ready," she said into it then listened. "Good timing." She hung up. "Let's get ready for—"

A knock sounded on the door behind them. Luca

glanced at Nella to make sure it was okay if she answered it.

"This is your place," Nella said, nodding as if she had heard Luca's question. "And I'm pretty sure it's your guide showing up to start that tour."

Wondering who that guide was—hoping it was a certain someone—Luca left Nicky with Nella and turned to go open the door.

Her hopes had been right. Mark stood there with Rocky "Hey, Luca." Wow, he knew her new name already. "Are you ready for a quick walk around the shelter?" he asked, his thick brows raised over his smiling blue eyes. "Not much time before lunch, but at least you'll get to see where things are. And maybe meet a few of the animals. Although I imagine any people will pass us in a hurry to get into the cafeteria. You'll have to meet them later."

Luca laughed. "Sounds good."

"And we'll get your things out of your car a little later," Mark said.

"Great," Luca replied, appreciating his help in advance. She turned to get Nicky, but he was already at her side, with Nella right beside him, her hands on his shoulders.

"Now you all run ahead," Nella said. "I'm heading downstairs to check on the meal fixings. Oh, and to eat too." She smiled then gently pushed Nicky toward the door.

Luca went out the door first, holding Nicky's hand. Mark turned, and he followed them, along with his dog.

The hallway remained empty. "Is this floor all occupied?" Luca asked as they walked to the elevator.

"As far as I know there are a few vacant apartments, but you're not the only ones here." He pushed the button.

The car arrived almost immediately and they got in. It didn't take long to get downstairs, and Mark hung back with Rocky as Luca walked her son into the wide, high-ceilinged entryway. The noisy wide entryway, since a soft roar of voices emanated from the cafeteria.

"Sounds as if there are a lot of hungry people in there," Luca said then hesitated. "We could do this later if you'd like to go eat. Or Nicky and I could just take a short walk on our own for now."

"Nope, quick tour first then food." Mark's grin was broad, somehow enhancing his handsome features even more. "But yeah, I'm hungry. Let's plan on eating soon."

A bunch of people walked into the building as they were exiting. Mark said hi and they reciprocated, as well as sent greetings to Nicky and Luca. Some patted Rocky too. Several seemed affectionate with her son as well and bent down to say hello directly to him. And sweet Nicky, being himself, said hi back.

They were mostly women, primarily older. Luca wondered who might be under the shelter's protection and suspected now that older women might be the most endangered.

But she wasn't so old. And she noticed some men, too, of different ages. And some of the people were also of different ethnicities.

She looked forward to meeting everyone here, as many as possible, although it might take some time.

Plus, she knew she would most likely never learn what had brought any of them here. That was a good thing. She didn't want to talk about her own circumstances either.

She held on to Nicky's hand as they eased by those approaching them. They were quickly at the end of the concrete walkway.

"Let's just make a quick visit to each of the buildings for now," Mark said. "Then we can come back."

"Sounds good to me."

In moments, they were striding with Rocky on his leash, in and out of the various single-story buildings along the walkway, striding through the long shelter areas with enclosures containing all dogs until the last building.

As with the enclosures in the small entry area, the dogs were all separated by size, with the toy and other small dogs in the first building, medium sized ones in the next, and then one with enclosures containing large dogs.

The last building had cats in enclosures along the sides. There was also a door at the back that led into a room occupied by gerbils, rabbits and guinea pigs.

Luca was impressed at how clean everything appeared to be. There were few bad smells in any of the buildings. She assumed she would be among those who helped to clean the buildings. She might even clean up after the animals—not her favorite thing, but it would be okay.

As they walked, Mark gave her some information about how things were handled at the shelter. Among other things, he told her that staff members also helped train the dogs, with guidance from managers and those who'd been there awhile. She loved that idea and hoped to make sure Nicky could watch, or even help.

She'd also noticed the security cameras hung outside the buildings here and there. That seemed in sync with the protective nature of the shelter. She wasn't thrilled that they were probably being videoed, but that was just the way things were.

And she knew that anything bad, anyone bad, would also be photographed. Although she trusted nothing bad would ever happen here.

Inside the buildings, as they'd hurried through, Nicky was thrilled to see the doggies and talk to them. "You'll get to play with some of them soon," Mark had told him, which had only excited him more.

In the last building, seeing the small animals in their cages, Nicky was excited. "Can I play with them soon too?" he asked.

"Not sure," Mark said. "I haven't seen anyone playing with them. We'll just have to see whether those in charge think it's a good idea."

Their quick tour through the shelter grounds over, they started back to where they had begun.

"Are you hungry, honey?" Luca asked her son.

"Yesssss," he replied as they walked, grasping her hand.

"That's a good thing," Mark said, looking down without slackening his pace. "You're about to get a really good lunch, Nicky. Lots of good food." He looked up at Luca, still walking quickly. "So will you. And you'll

Chapter 4

As they neared the building that held their apartment and the dining area downstairs, Nicky started skipping quickly toward it, which amused Mark. Cute kid. Looked great in his shelter T-shirt. And he was apparently hungry.

Luca, also in a shelter T-shirt, quickened her pace, too, to stay nearer her son. Mark, with Rocky, kept up with both of them. Not that it was necessary for him to introduce them to the staffers inside the cafeteri— his current assignment was to give them a tour and help get things out of Luca's car, while getting to observe how that shirt hugged her curves and—

No. None of that.

Anyway, intros wouldn't hurt. Plus, he could watch the reactions of the staff members to the newbies, as he watched their reactions to everything else.

get to meet some of the people who prepared it, as well as others who'll join us for lunch. I think we'll all have an enjoyable time."

And here, under the protection of this shelter, of this man, and knowing they could stay for a while, Luca felt sure she would have a lot more than an enjoyable time.

That was his real purpose here, after all: keeping an eye on everyone and everything to figure out if any threats were emanating from inside the shelter's all-enclosing walls.

They soon entered the dining area. It was a large room, with long, parallel tables in the middle, each with beige tablecloths. A perpendicular table at the end held food, cafeteria-style. A beverage table sat beside that one, holding water, some soft drinks and coffee.

A lot of people were already seated at the tables and there was a lineup for the serving table. Mark pondered where they should sit, and who he should introduce Luca to first, noting the hum of conversations around them from those present.

As he often did here, he tied Rocky's leash to a chair near the door, where his dog wouldn't get in people's way but could help protect the place. The dogs who lived at the shelter were back in their confined areas there.

As he walked by the tables with his human companions, quite a few people looked at Nicky. Mark understood they weren't used to seeing youngsters around here. Not that he'd been here long, but Mark had learned from Scott that Nicky would be the first child since the shelter opened.

Where they stood, he couldn't pick up any aromas from the food. Dinners were more fragrant usually, when roasts, casseroles and more were served, but lunches were mostly sandwiches and soups that weren't home-made but still served from large pots.

"Should we just get in line?" Luca asked him.

"That's the best approach," he said. "You'll soon see

why people like to eat the food here and not just hang out in their own apartments."

He wondered who was in the kitchen organizing things. He did see Nella near the doorway. Luca had already met her, so no need for introductions there.

When they got in line, the people right in front of them included Chessie, Denise and Bibi. All wore the standard Chance Animal Shelter T-shirts as well as jeans of different shades of blue and lengths.

Bibi spoke first. She was a somewhat large lady, clearly happy for lunchtime, and when she smiled, a gap between her front teeth was her most obvious feature.

"Hello, newcomers," she said. "And welcome, especially to this little guy." She bent and widened her grin even more toward Nicky. "Hi. I hope you're hungry. We've got lots of good food. Are you hungry?"

Nicky nodded. "Yes," he said shyly.

"Well, you won't be for much longer. What's your name?"

"It's Nicky," Luca said before he could answer.

Mark wondered if his mother had explained to the boy that he'd be called something else from now on, and what her rationale had been. Did he get it? Would he respond to Nicky?

Mark figured he'd find out soon.

"Hi, Nicky," Bibi said, and at least the boy didn't contradict her. "I'm Bibi. And you're—" She looked up at Luca.

"I'm Luca. Great to meet you, Bibi."

"And I'm Denise," said the woman in line between them. "I'm happy to meet you, Luca and Nicky."

and remained alive, and ended up here. Still cooking. A good thing? Well, the food she made seemed good to Mark, and no one had gotten ill from it.

Luca stood there for a minute, apparently scanning the tables for seats.

"Over there," Mark suggested, waving with his free hand toward a table nearer the entry door that didn't appear full. He scanned who was there and figured they'd be fine with a newcomer and her kid.

Who wouldn't be, around here? Something different was always exciting to the residents, as long as no danger was involved. And Luca certainly didn't appear dangerous.

Once again, he noted that the people they passed seemed focused on watching the little guy.

They sat at the end of the table, with Mark facing Nicky and Luca, after heading over to give Rocky, who'd been sitting there watching, a reassuring pat on the head. Beside him was Kathy, a senior who was very thin. She was pretty good at training dogs too.

Nicky sat in the last chair across from him. And on Luca's other side was Gordon, whom Mark understood was a relative newcomer to the shelter. He was one of the many whose backgrounds Mark didn't know. He was a senior. He had wisps of black hair on his head, a bit of dark stubble on his thin face, and eyes that he apparently had to convince to look into other people's faces. Mark figured he'd had a pretty difficult background to have landed him here.

All of them wore Chance Animal Shelter shirts, of course.

The meal progressed well. Mark wasn't surprised to see Scott enter the dining room with Nella, and another manager, Campbell, known as "Camp," was with them.

Mark watched little Nicky eat his half sandwich with gusto, nearly finishing it. He talked to Nicky a lot, as did Luca, asking him what he thought of the food and if he'd like to see some more doggies after they were done.

He absolutely did.

Now, all Mark needed to do was to figure out when and where there'd be a training session so the child could see some dogs and handlers in action. He wasn't sure about Gordon's abilities, but he had seen Kathy do some training, so he asked her.

"I don't suppose you'll be working with a few of our dog residents this afternoon, will you? I think it would be great to show Nicky a training session."

He felt good under the smile Luca shot at him. He felt even better when Kathy said, "Oh, yes, I'd already planned on doing some training. Nicky can definitely watch."

As they finished, a couple of staffers came over to say hello. "Who's this?" asked Muriel, one of the people Mark had seen work the most with the dogs, a pretty lady in her thirties with a deep-colored complexion.

"This is Nicky," Mark said then quickly had an idea.

First, though, he looked across the table to ask Luca if it was all right with her if he gave a general intro-duction of Nicky to the whole group of people in the cafeteria.

"I guess so," she said. "It won't put him in any dan-ger, will it?"

"I believe that people knowing who he is will help protect him, but it's up to you."

"Okay," she said. "But…well, would you ask Scott?"

"That's what I intended to do next." He rose and went to a table a couple of rows away where Scott sat with Nella and some of the staffers. He told Scott what he hoped to do, since so many people there had seemed curious about the child.

"It's okay with me if Luca's all right with it."

"She seemed fine as long as you're all right with it."

Scott smiled. "Fine then. Guess no one around here is used to seeing kids, so we might as well let them know that an occasional child here is okay."

Mark went back to Luca and Nicky and asked that they accompany him for the introduction. Since Scott had clearly said yes, Luca agreed and they walked among the tables till they reached the end of the room.

Rocky stood and wagged his long tail. Smiling, Mark patted his sweet K-9 on the head again, then banged on the wall to make enough noise for people to notice, which they did.

He figured some would be a bit unnerved by the unexpected sound, considering the protective circumstances that had brought them here.

Luca didn't look pleased, but she didn't say anything. Nicky also appeared concerned, but Mark told him to bang on the wall, too, which he did, and grinned.

Then Mark called out to the rest of the room. "Sorry for the noise, everyone, but a lot of you have noticed one of our latest staff members, a very young one. I got the okay to introduce him to you."

Everyone had grown silent. Some did look worried, but at Mark's explanation of what he was up to, most seemed to relax. Some even smiled.

"I'd like you all to meet Nicky. He's going to help us out here by assisting in animal care, and he will hopefully learn to do some dog training too. Nicky, say hi to everyone."

The little guy's brown eyes lit up and he started waving as he turned in what appeared to be an attempt to see the whole crowd, which was probably around twenty people. "Hi to everyone," he shouted with a big grin.

Laughs erupted around them, including from Mark and Luca.

"Okay," Mark said, "Feel free to say hi to Nicky and his mom, Luca, when you see them around. And you can help Nicky learn what he needs to so he can be with the dogs and other animals more, which is what he'd like to do. Right, Nicky?"

Would he respond to being called Nicky? Once again, he came across as being a smart kid, since he didn't attempt to correct Mark. "Right. I like animals. I like doggies."

"We all do around here, good little guy," Mark said. "And I think you'll get to see some go to work this afternoon. But right now, give Rocky a pat and you and your mom can sit back down to finish your lunch."

The meal was nice but a bit overwhelming with all the people around, Luca thought after they'd finished eating and went out the door. She'd waited until most of the other diners had left, which had allowed Nicky to eat an extra cookie and sip his glass of water. Mark had remained with them, Rocky at his side, as they'd paused on the walkway.

Still, they'd all been so sweet, especially to Nicky. The food was fine. And it had certainly been a good way to meet some of the others in protective custody, as she and her four-year-old were now.

She'd seen people head upstairs toward the apartments, but now she watched others enter the shelter buildings. A few had already come out with dogs on leashes, apparently walking them.

Luca wasn't sure where she and Nicky should go. But they were at a pet shelter. She wanted to make her son as happy as possible. Could they visit some of the animals?

Mark seemed to have read her mind. "So," he said, "let's go into one of the buildings. I think we'll find Kathy in the first one, where the toy dogs are. She can introduce us to some, and then we should be able to watch her do some training."

"Sounds great!" Luca said. "Right, Nicky?"

Fortunately, her son had accepted the game she'd told him they were playing, where they'd be answering to the new names they'd been given. He seemed to like the name Nicky well enough. But he was glad he could still call her "Mommy."

"Yes, Mommy," he said, his tone excited as he jumped up and down. "Doggies!"

They headed for the enclosures where Luca knew the smallest dogs were kept, closest to the cafeteria and apartment building. As they opened the door to enter,

Chessie appeared with a little white, somewhat shaggy dog that looked like part poodle.

"Hi. I'm walking Oodles. Do you want to pet him?" she asked Nicky.

"Yes!" he said vehemently. Chessie walked the pup outside and stood near the door, while Nicky played with him, petting him and pushing him gently. Fortunately, the little dog was friendly.

"He's a good dog," Chessie confirmed. "I didn't plan this, but he's a perfect little pup for Nicky to play with."

"That's great," Luca said. "Thanks."

"But we have to get on our walk." And so they did, with Nicky watching somewhat sadly.

"Hey, let's go inside and see who else you can meet," Mark said as he and Rocky led them back inside.

Luca couldn't help smiling at all the small dogs she saw immediately, maybe ten of them. They were in a long row of enclosures, with concrete floors like the outer area and raised platforms inside, complete with fluffy dog beds and food and water bowls on the floor. The dogs were of all different colors and sizes, though all small, and seemed excited to have the humans visit them.

Kathy stood at the farthest enclosure. She reached over the chain-link fence to pet some pups in there.

"Hi," she said. "I want to introduce you to a couple of my favorites, then we'll take one outside for a walk and do a little training class, okay?"

"Okay!" Nicky said right away.

Luca loved the idea too. She was happy to watch her

son pet a cute Jack Russell lookalike named Jack but was glad the energetic pup wasn't the one Kathy chose.

There were a couple others, too, but the one Kathy removed when she opened the gate was a small brown terrier mix. Kathy closed the gate and picked up the dog, bending so Nicky could pet him. "This is Mocha," she said, snapping on a leash. "He's been here for a while, so I'm spending extra time to give him attention and training so he'll be ready for someone to finally adopt him. Want to help me?"

"Yes," Nicky said, holding out his hand for Luca as Kathy started walking the dog down the hall.

"Oh, don't you want to help?" she asked, turning around to look at Nicky.

"Yes!" Nicky said again and joined her.

Kathy looked at Luca as if asking if it was okay, so she nodded. Kathy then handed Nicky the leash but kept hold of it, too, walking both child and dog through the rest of the building to the door, where she led them outside.

Luca was amused but not surprised to see several other staff members exercising dogs nearby, some a lot larger than Mocha. She figured Nicky would want to meet some of those pups, too, which was fine as long as someone in charge could tell her which were safe for a youngster to pet.

Mark and Rocky started walking with Kathy and her companions. That was a good thing, Luca decided. Not that she expected cute little Mocha to get nasty, but nice Mark and his sweet, large Doberman would protect Nicky too. Luca appreciated that. A lot.

But enough of that. Kathy would also take care of Nicky, Luca assumed, since she had taken him under her wing for this walk.

Only, she stopped near the end of the building and had Mocha and Nicky walk along the narrow sidewalk perpendicular to the longer one. What was she doing?

Training the dog, as it turned out. Asking Nicky to release the leash, she had Mocha's attention, evidently readying the pup to start obeying some standard dog commands like sit, down and stay.

Mocha watched her closely and obeyed them all.

Smart little dog. And clearly well trained already. But it never hurt to practice and learn more.

Luca was amused when Kathy had Nicky give some of the commands, which he did with gusto. Sure enough, Mocha did sit and stay and lie down for him. Even gave him his paw.

Luca clapped quietly, wanting to cheer. Feeling happy that her son seemed to be enjoying himself.

Feeling even happier that they were here, under this shelter's protection. They were safe, at least for now.

She glanced at Mark, who stood beside her, also watching the training show. He was smiling as well, and he nodded to her as if he knew what was on her mind. She appreciated his attitude.

Okay, realistically she appreciated him in many ways—although liking his looks, his sexy cowboy attitude at times, even when he wasn't wearing the hat, was totally inappropriate.

Well, he didn't have to know about her feelings. They

were undoubtedly just an offshoot of her relief that she and her son had found a safe place to stay.

"Good training session," he said. "Looks as if Nicky is cut out to be a dog trainer, at least while he's here. Maybe you should learn all about it too."

"I'd like that," she said. "And to learn anything else about helping to keep the animals safe and get them adopted into new forever homes fast."

"The faster the better," Mark acknowledged, "as long as all the safety protocols for pets and people are followed."

"Then I need to learn more about all of them," Luca said. "What's the best way to learn?"

"You can always talk to our managers. Or to me. I don't know it all, since I'm still learning, but I know more than you about this place, at least for now."

Luca knew she would rely on Mark for at least some of what she needed.

She'd already started to do so. Too much.

Or maybe not enough.

But whichever, she definitely appreciated his presence.

Chapter 5

Mark watched for a bit while Luca and Nicky worked with Kathy as she trained Mocha. He enjoyed hanging out with the newcomers. But he had things to do that afternoon, and Luca now knew some people here in addition to Kathy, who seemed to have taken charge of training Nicky too.

He leaned over slightly as she watched the training lesson. "Got some stuff I need to do now, but I'll see you later." He figured no explanation was necessary, especially since he couldn't tell her the truth.

She was caught up anyway in watching what her son was doing with the pup and real trainer, so he was a little surprised when she turned to look at him. "Okay. Will you join us for dinner? Or before?" The expression on her lovely face appeared worried, as if it made a difference whether she saw him again by then.

That made him feel better than it should have.

But maybe she didn't feel as comfortable here with what was going on.

"Certainly for dinner," he said. "And you can be sure there'll be other staff members out here who work on training, not just dog walking, so you and Nicky can start learning from them too."

"Okay." She pressed her lips together and shook her head. "Sorry. I didn't mean to sound pushy, but you've been so kind to us in circumstances that could have been really difficult, even though just being here is so helpful. I really appreciate it." She shook her head and looked down, apparently embarrassed.

Not what he wanted her to feel, though caring for him wouldn't be appropriate either. "Hey, don't worry about it. I'm glad to have met Nicky and you before anyone else around here did, and I want to help you any way I can." And keep an eye on her for multiple reasons. "But you'll see. There are lots of good people here."

And some not so good? He hoped not, although looking into the possibility was why he was really there.

Not that he'd even hint at that to Luca.

"I know. And I want to get to know you all better. Everyone's been so sweet to Nicky. But—okay, I don't want to rely on anyone too much. Especially you. So have a good afternoon, whatever you're up to, and hopefully we'll see you later." She reached down and patted Rocky on his head. Mark's good dog wagged his tail.

What I'm up to is something else to ensure your safety, and the others' too, he thought, but he wasn't about to mention that.

Nor that he'd be leaving the shelter for a while.

But first he needed to talk to Scott.

"You'll definitely see us later," he said. He waved at Nicky, who was too busy raising his hand to try to get Mocha to sit to look his direction. Then Mark headed toward the office building with Rocky.

Would Luca wonder why he was going in there? Maybe, but he could always make up something about needing to talk to one of the managers about a minor question or issue. That was actually true, although the issue could be major.

He entered the building and walked upstairs to the floor where Scott's office was, as he had earlier that day. He passed the first door to an unused office, plus the additional managers' offices, then knocked on the door that was Scott's.

The director opened the door in a few seconds. "I figured it was you."

Scott gestured, and Mark entered the office. He sat on the chair he'd occupied before lunch, Rocky lying down beside his feet.

"So," he said as Scott also took his seat. "I assume it's time for me to head downtown again, but is there anything I should know this time?"

Mark had sneaked out and gone to the police station a few times since he'd started his undercover assignment to talk to his superiors. That was the routine they'd established in the short time he'd lived at the shelter—Scott, the law enforcement chiefs and him. Although they worried whether any staff members would see him leave, they'd developed a story about what a bad guy he was as a staff member, sneakily taking his dog for walks outside.

If he was ever caught, he'd let whoever found him know he wasn't about to bring anyone else along on the walk. He would say he'd left so he could walk Rocky somewhere other than inside the restrictive facility.

That, in a way, was true, but not the real reason.

"I'm not aware of anything specific this time," Scott told him as Mark eyed with envy his slightly more formal Chance Animal Shelter work shirt. It looked more Western than the T-shirts. "I've spoken with Assistant Chief Kara a little, and she said the gossip in town about strange things has slowed down. For now at least.

"As you and I have talked about a lot, we've heard about rumors before. Though we work hard to keep our real purpose secret, speculations sometimes zing around. Although, people still do come here to drop off unwanted animals and to adopt pets too. But—as Kara's told us, she's just waiting for the next time there are issues. Nice lady that she is, she's concerned about our ongoing safety, and so's Chief Shermovski. That's why you're here—to figure out what's real and what isn't. But I know you need their information and guidance. So, yes, it's a good thing you're heading to town even if there's nothing specific at the moment. Maybe you'll come up with additional ideas about how to keep things this quiet."

"Hope so," Mark said. His prior visits with his superiors at the police station had only made him more concerned. But even when rumors were floating around, they hadn't been able to provide him with any helpful information—other than it seemed like some of the problems, some of the rumors, might be a result of one or more staff members getting word out regarding what the supersecret shelter for people in trouble was really about. Hence, Mark's undercover assignment to try to ferret out something helpful about one or more of the staffers, which he hadn't so far. And it sounded like this downtown trek would be just as useless as his prior ones, especially because there were fewer concerns at the moment. But just in case…

"Okay," he said. "Thanks for the update, even if there's not much to update about. I'll get on my way."

"Good. And let me know tonight the result of your conversations."

"Will do."

Mark and Rocky left, heading down the stairs. He had an urge to go say a temporary goodbye again to Luca, which he quashed immediately. He also had an urge to return to his apartment for his hat and boots, but he'd be too obvious that way, even more than he otherwise was. He always appreciated growing up in San Antonio, Texas, as part of a family that encouraged acting like a cowboy since his long-ago ancestors had in fact been out on the range herding cattle. Or so he'd been told by his proud paternal grandpa. He hadn't met anyone further back than that, but Grandpa Martindale was one of his favorite relatives. He and Grandma had lived in a home in a nice suburban development that resembled an actual ranch house, and little Clark, still using his real name then, had naturally loved to visit.

He'd joined the San Antonio PD, then been recruited

into the Sacramento, California, police force, which was where he became a K-9 cop. That was also where he'd been when he'd been asked to participate in this very special project.

He reported to the officers in charge at the Chance PD, as he was an undercover member of that police force as a K-9 cop, but hardly anyone knew it.

Right now, he and Rocky proceeded in the direction they usually used to sneak out.

Going through the cafeteria allowed some degree of secrecy in leaving. There was an exit there that people didn't use much, although sometimes food was brought in that way.

A couple staff members were inside cleaning up, but he edged around them so he and his dog weren't seen, walked down some stairs and looked on the floor behind the last stairwell where he always hid his non-shelter black T-shirt. Yay. It was there. So was Rocky's halter, which should give his dog more comfort than having a leash hooked to his collar as they trekked for a while.

He quickly exchanged shirts and stuck his Chance Animal Shelter shirt where he'd retrieved the other one from. He put the halter on Rocky and hooked the leash to it.

He also made sure his cell phone was in his pocket. Yes, he had one, even though the staff members here weren't supposed to. He kept it well hidden and only used it when no one else was around. The number was a new one, not one he'd had before his identity was changed.

Then, unlocking and relocking some doors, he sneaked

outside, where he also unlocked a gate in the tall wooden fence and edged into the rear parking area with Rocky.

He glanced around and was glad to see no one around, people or cars. He quickly crossed the road into the park across from the rear of the shelter, ignoring the sports gear and hardware stores down the street.

Then they started their walk, on the grassy area and, better yet, among the trees.

Was this all much too obvious? He kept attempting to remain as secret as possible, but he figured someday someone inappropriate would notice him. Still, he could play the role of a shelter resident who was sneaky enough to get out. That's what he was, after all.

It was just why he was a shelter resident, his real role in sneaking around, and why he did it, that were the secret things.

And as an undercover cop, he considered himself a damn good liar. He could hopefully talk his way out of anything.

Although he hoped he wouldn't have to.

The hike took a while to get to the civic center in downtown Chance since he kept changing directions to try to avoid being noticed, or followed, even though there were other pedestrians around, some also walking dogs. He hoped he looked like one of those civilians.

Then he started walking proudly with his dog in the vicinity of the police station. He figured he didn't look particularly like a K-9 cop at the moment, nor did he appear to be a Chance Animal Shelter staff member.

He hoped. And he doubted anyone was paying enough attention to him for him to worry.

Although they might pay attention to his sweet Dobie. At least Rocky only had a halter on, not an official vest of any type.

In a short while, though, after scrutinizing people walking along the street to see if they were looking at him—which some appeared to be, although they were all watching Rocky rather than the human with him—Mark headed for the back of the station, calling Kara to let her know he was about to arrive.

He would still be Mark here. Those he worked with were aware of his undercover identity, and the decision had been to continue to call him by his current name, both to help him recall who he was but also to ensure he wasn't officially identified while visiting here.

Although those who knew him as a cop would identify him that way anyhow.

Civilians weren't supposed to enter from the rear door.

Also, civilians didn't have keys to enter there, which Mark did.

Once inside the narrow hallway, he was met not by Assistant Police Chief Kara Province, but by her superior officer, Chief Andrew Shermovski, known as "Sherm."

"You're here to talk to Kara, right?" he asked Mark in a low voice.

Sherm was in his sixties. He had wrinkles on his face, and salt-and-pepper hair, but his build looked solid. He wore the standard uniform around here, white shirt and black trousers, although sometimes the officers also wore a jacket. Sherm's shirt had some medals and patches on it too.

"That's right," Mark said. "Although I'm here to see if there's anything new I should know about. Do you know of anything?"

"Nope. And I suspect Kara hasn't heard anything lately either. When she and I talked—and yes, she told me you were coming and asked me to meet you—she had more questions than information."

Great, Mark thought. *This might be a wasted venture*.

But it was never wasted when he kept in contact with those who could provide help if he ever needed it.

And who also might come up with answers he couldn't.

"Care to join us even if we don't have anything new to talk about?" Mark asked as a couple of uniformed cops walked by, a man and woman. Not unexpectedly, they looked at Rocky rather than at Mark, then continued past in the narrow hallway.

"Sounds good to me," Sherm said. "In fact, Kara already invited me, when she asked me to meet you here."

Mark laughed. "Why am I not surprised?"

"Because you're smart." Sherm began leading them in the same direction the other cops had gone.

When they went through the door, they were at the back of the large interior station area, where the elevators were. They were soon on their way to the third floor.

Another police officer was on the elevator with them,

a young man who was probably a rookie. "Hello, sir," he said to Sherm when they entered the elevator.

"Hello, Officer," Sherm responded.

The cop quickly moved his attention to the real star in the car. "What a nice dog," he said to Mark.

"Yes, he is," Mark responded.

They finally reached their destination, got off the elevator and quickly walked down the hall to Kara's office. Mark didn't pay attention to where the young officer headed after giving Rocky a quick pat on the head.

Sherm knocked on the door and they walked in. Kara's office was fairly large, although the chief's, which Mark had seen, was larger. "Hello, gentlemen," she said. "And Rocky." Like many other people, she moved to pat Rocky gently on the head. As he always did, Mark's dog stood there, apparently enjoying the attention since he wagged his tail.

Kara wore the same uniform as Sherm but looked a lot different in it. She was a slim woman and somewhat tall. Her hair was short and black, her eyes brown. Yes, she looked like a cop, a professional, but a lot more attractive than her boss.

That didn't matter to Mark. What did matter was her expertise as a cop in charge.

And her intelligence and ability to find the kind of information all of them in this office needed to learn for Mark to do his job and to defend the protective shelter where he was undercover.

"Have a seat," she said after petting Rocky, gesturing toward the black chairs on the wooden floor across from her desk, which had a bunch of folders on it, all in neat piles. A laptop computer sat on a table off to the side of her comfortable-looking desk chair.

Mark obeyed. He considered immediately leaping into the situation, demanding that Kara tell him why she thought things had grown quiet. He'd been hired to help because of what might have been threats. It would be good if they'd stopped, but he'd like to know why.

At least there seemed no reason to suspect Luca of anything, though Mark would include her in his investigation.

Were some staff members at the shelter getting ready to harm it by letting the world know what it was really about?

Or were their concerns unnecessary?

Not that Mark had been involved long, but he understood from talking to these police chiefs, and Scott, too, that menacing things had occurred at least a couple times since the shelter had opened over a year ago now.

Fortunately, whatever had gotten out had been taken care of and kept quiet, so the shelter hadn't been harmed.

Several people involved in those situations had been caught and incarcerated in places where whatever they said wouldn't get far, and wouldn't be believed anyway.

So what was happening now?

But before he could start questioning these highly placed law enforcement folks, Kara said, "It's good to see you here, Mark. Rocky too. And you're following our current precedent by coming today. But things have been quiet recently. No rumors we've heard about the shelter. No threats. Has anything occurred there that we should know about?"

"Not that I'm aware of," he said. "We got a new staff member. Two, in a way. Our new staffer brought her four-year-old son with her."

"How cute!" Kara said.

"Even cuter is that he appears to like animals, and at least one of the staffers is helping him learn to train dogs."

Sherm let out a hoot and clapped his hands. "Sounds highly appropriate. Maybe they need more kiddos."

"Maybe so. I've heard there's been some online interest about a couple of the dogs, so we may have possible adopters show up to meet them. Maybe that could include ones the little guy has been helping with."

"Well, keep us informed," Kara said. "But I'm afraid your visit here today only put you in danger of being seen leaving without giving you a good reason to do so."

"Maybe I'm not needed there after all." Mark hated to say that. He liked being there. He hoped he'd in some way be useful. Besides showing Luca and Nicky around.

Fortunately, Sherm recognized his presence was potentially a good thing.

"I doubt things are quiet just because you're there," he said. "And you need to hang out there for a while to keep an eye on things and your ears open to what the staff members are saying. There were rumors floating around downtown here for a while without a source being identified. The fact they've stopped doesn't mean any danger has ended."

"Exactly," Kara said. "We need you there, Mark. And

we need you to stop in here every few days so you can keep us up to date about what you see and hear. Even if it's nothing."

"I get it," he said. "Maybe Rocky's presence keeps the staff members in line." He looked down at his K-9. "And—well, like you, I don't feel entirely comfortable about whatever was going on before simply stopping. We need to know what it was about."

"Absolutely." Kara rose and came over again to pat Rocky. She was obviously a dog person, even though she was an assistant police chief and not a K-9 cop.

Mark waited a while, smiling as he watched, and Sherm aimed a smile at him, too, over Kara's head.

But after a minute, the chief said, "So will you head back to the shelter now?"

"Yep, unless you think there's anything else we should discuss now," Mark confirmed. "Carefully, as usual. And I'll try to listen to what's in the heads of people we pass in case any of the rumors that happened before came from any of them."

Kara laughed and returned to her seat. "Yeah, you do that. And be sure to let us know. In fact, can you hear what's in our heads?"

Mark nodded. "Same as what's in mine. Relief. And frustration. And worry about what's next. Right?"

"You got it," Kara replied.

Chapter 6

Luca loved watching her son be taught how to work with dogs in training, even though he was too young to do a whole lot.

But Kathy was great, working with Mocha and Nicky beside the small dog building.

And soon one of the other staff members, who introduced himself as Leonard, came over and suggested that Kathy join him in another area of the yard, where he said more training sessions were held. He had Jack with him, the energetic Jack Russell terrier mix they had met before.

They all walked to the center paved area, where Leonard stopped in a grassy patch near the small dog building, with Jack leashed at his side. Other staff members walked by with various dogs, but for the moment none joined them to work on training. Would they train their dogs later? Had they worked with them before? Or were they just giving them attention?

Luca figured she would learn more about how things worked around here the longer Nicky and she stayed.

As she'd started doing with the people she met here, Luca wondered about Leonard's background. Kathy's too. They were very different, and not just because one was male and the other female.

Leonard appeared to be in his early twenties, maybe even a bit younger. He had longish brown hair, twinkling brown eyes, and seemed very lithe as he worked with Jack—a good idea since the terrier had so much energy. What danger had brought this young man here? Luca doubted she'd find out, which was fine since she didn't want him, or anyone else here, to learn her background.

Kathy, on the other hand, was an older lady, at least in her sixties. She was very thin, but she had energy and seemed supple, too, as she walked with Mocha, who also had some vigor despite not being as active as Jack.

Leonard was the first to give the dog in his control some commands, firmly but nicely, and energetic Jack seemed to love it. It didn't hurt that Leonard gave him treats as he calmly obeyed, although the staffer didn't overdo it.

Same went for Kathy when she began to work with Mocha again.

And both staff members seemed thrilled to show Nicky what they were doing and to work with him to get the dogs to do basics like sit, stay and down, things

Kathy had already demonstrated. He seemed thrilled to attempt to have the dogs obey him.

And all of it thrilled Luca as well.

"It's so much fun to watch your training," Luca couldn't help saying. "And the dogs seem so willing to be trained, and even to work with Nicky."

"Yeah, they've both been here for a while, like we have," Leonard said.

Really? How long had he been at the shelter?

Kathy, too, for that matter.

Did either want to find a new life somewhere else? Or were they so worried about what had happened to them before that they figured they'd stay in protective custody forever—even young Leonard?

Okay, she was being too curious for a staff member here, Luca scolded herself. At least she wasn't asking any questions.

"They've been here too long," Leonard went on. "The idea is for the animals here to be adopted into their forever homes as soon as possible. I've been in the reception area when some potential adopters come in to see our shelter dogs and have been really excited to see some of the happy results."

"Me too," Kathy said, a smile lighting her face.

"I hope we get to see it too," Luca said. "I'll bet Nicky would be really happy to see one of his new doggy friends like Jack get a new person as a mommy or daddy."

She watched as her son, who was still working with Jack under Leonard's control, stopped and looked at her. "But does that mean Jack wouldn't be here anymore?" His lower lip quivered and he looked like he might cry.

"Yes," she acknowledged. "But he'd be so happy to have a new home and a person who loved him. And there are lots of other doggies here, plus new ones come in all the time, right?"

"That's right," said a voice from behind Luca. She turned to see Scott standing there. And, yes, there were still staffers walking on the pathway with dogs of different sizes on leashes. Luca had been so caught up in the training that she'd lost track of other things going on around them.

Here, inside the shelter, that should be okay, she thought.

"A couple of staff members are visiting one of the nearby animal shelters tomorrow," Scott continued. "And they intend to bring some adoptable dogs and cats back with them. Maybe someday you two can go along on one of those visits and help choose who's likely to find new homes after living here and being trained by some staffers. Would you like that?" He seemed to address the question to Nicky, who'd fortunately become interested in the conversation and eased up on his worrying about possibly not seeing Jack again.

That made Luca very happy.

"Yes," he said solemnly. "I'd like that."

"Well, let's see what we can work out, hopefully sometime soon. But right now—" The director turned toward Luca. "I've got a couple things I'd like to talk to you about. Can you come to my office?"

"Sure," she said, wondering what he had on his mind. "Nicky, we need to leave the doggies for now."

"Please no, Mommy," he said, looking at her pleadingly with his sad brown eyes. "I want to help teach them."

"But, honey—"

Before she could finish, Leonard said, "I'll help him learn to teach them more. And I can keep an eye on him till you get back here. Okay?"

"I can watch him too," Kathy added. "It's fine for you to go to Scott's office. We'll be here when you get back."

Luca knew she had come to this place because of the protection Nicky and she would receive. But the idea of leaving her son with others, without her own presence, worried her.

On the other hand, these people were under protection, too, and knew what it was like to be concerned about safety.

And they both seemed to give a damn about Nicky, about helping her son learn to work with dogs, at least.

Plus, there were two of them, so they could keep an eye on each other as well as Nicky.

"Okay," she finally said. "Thanks. I won't be long." She aimed a gaze toward Scott to make sure he was okay with that, and he nodded.

And so, with an uncertain smile, Luca bent to give her son a hug, then rose to follow the director.

They headed down the walkway toward the main buildings and entered the one containing offices. Luca had been there earlier to see if she could stay and sign the paperwork. This time, she headed up the wooden stairway behind Scott.

Soon they were on the top floor and Scott led her past

the closed doors for which Luca's earlier presumption of their being managers' offices had been confirmed.

In a short while, she occupied a chair in Scott's office, facing his desk, where he now sat.

She looked at the director, wondering what this visit was about. Were she and her son about to be booted out of the shelter for some reason?

Had the danger against them increased?

Had her enemy, Morley, determined where they were?

It turned out to be none of the above.

"I wanted to let you know," he said, "that Mitzi has been in touch with me. Your friend remains concerned about how you and your son are doing and has, in a very nice way, been urging me to put you in touch with her so she can confirm with you what I've told her.

"I did tell her the two of you were here, that you've been given new identities and an apartment of your own, and you'll be able to stay here for as long as it takes to figure out where you should be. She says she gets it, and it complies with the little she's heard about our facility, but she still wants you to corroborate. And she also knows that you aren't permitted to have a phone or to leave for a meeting."

Luca nodded, not sure what to say except, "Well, I'm not sure how we can communicate—email maybe?— but I'd be happy to talk to her and give her an update. A careful update, since I know I'm not supposed to talk about this shelter or what goes on here. But I could tell her that what you've said about Nicky—or is she not supposed to learn our new names?"

"Yes, that's fine. If she communicates more, it's better that she uses your current identities with us, although she needs to agree not to let anyone else know. I've explained that to her and she seems fine with it."

"Got it. Then I can let her know that 'Nicky and Luca' are here and doing fine, and appreciate all that's being done for us. But how—"

"As you suggested," Scott interjected, "email should be the way. But I'll set you up with a new email address, and that's the only one you should use. You shouldn't even check your former emails, even though it's different from using a cell phone with GPS that can be used to track you. But it's better if no one from your past can contact you at all unless I approve it."

Luca considered that, leaning back somewhat in the not entirely comfortable plastic chair. Since the loss of her husband, and his partner's subsequent obsession with her—and her concern that that obsession had started earlier and had caused said partner to be the murderer—she didn't think she wanted to be in touch with most people from her past anyway. Her parents and brother knew she, and her son, were in protective custody somewhere without knowing any information about it. They were fully aware that she couldn't contact them, at least for now, and that they shouldn't talk to anyone about her.

Mitzi, who'd helped her so much, was a good exception to those she couldn't stay in contact with.

"I understand. But it's okay to be in touch with Mitzi?"

"Not a lot. Right now, it will be fine, but even that

needs to have limits. She might not intentionally indicate anything to Morley, your enemy, but it's better to risk it as little as possible. Yes, she knows a lot about where you are and why, since she helped to get you here, so she could reveal it all if she ever chose to, or even do it accidentally. That is a good reason not to stay in close touch with her."

That sounded sad to Luca. On the other hand, she'd known, coming here, that she wouldn't be able to be in contact with her past, or anyone in it, maybe forever.

But it would be good to get in touch with Mitzi this once and to let her know that her much-appreciated assistance had put Luca and Nicky in a really good place. That, hopefully, their future, whatever it might be, would be safe.

"I'll handle things in whatever way you say," Luca told Scott, looking into blue eyes that were boring into her as if expecting some kind of response like that. He was a nice-looking guy. Luca had noticed that before. But he was so serious around her, so solemn, that his handsomeness was irrelevant to her. Apparently not to Nella though. Luca had already guessed, based on what she'd witnessed over the lunch hour, that the two of them, director and manager, were an item.

"Great. So—let's get you onto a computer in one of the manager's offices, one not occupied now so you'll have a little privacy. For now."

Really? He'd let her have a little privacy, even temporarily? She figured he would want to look over her shoulder and make sure that whatever she said to Mitzi in her email wouldn't be something she wasn't allowed to reveal.

"That sounds great," she said.

"Don't let any other staff member know though," he said as he stood and led her into the hall. "It's very rare that I give access to any computer, let alone in privacy. But this is a different situation than most staffers experience even when authorities introduce them to this place. Your Mitzi friend was very helpful, and now she's being very insistent. I think a brief communication with her will be okay. And let her know I okayed it and am aware what you're doing but it can't continue. And please don't overdo it."

"I understand." Even though Luca had just arrived at the shelter that day, her mind sadly filled with ideas of being here a long time with no one to talk to or to otherwise communicate with than the people in the shelter.

That wasn't necessarily a bad idea, she mused—and her mind jumped to picture Mark. She immediately erased his face from her thoughts.

Meanwhile, Scott led her outside his office and to one a couple of doors down. He didn't use a key card to unlock it, and she assumed that on this floor not everything was locked as many things below were.

The room was unsurprisingly smaller than Scott's office. It was sparsely furnished with a desk that had a chair behind it and a laptop on top, plus an extra chair facing it. The walls were blank, and the window at one side of the desk had a beige drapery pulled closed. Luca assumed it looked toward the apartment building.

There was no phone on the desk, not a surprise. Most

people and organizations used cell phones these days, although Luca was a bit sorry that she wouldn't be able to call anyone, especially from a place where whomever she called wouldn't know where she was, and couldn't use the number to track her with GPS.

But who would she dare call besides Mitzi anyway? And she'd soon be in touch with her via email.

"Now, let me get you set up," Mark said. He sat on the desk chair and began working with the laptop, his brow stern as he watched the screen. In a while, he stood. "I have it arranged so you can get right into email. I've set you up with a new email address that no one should recognize has anything to do with you, although I did let Mitzi know I'd be doing that, so she'll probably check all her emails until she finds yours."

"Sounds good. What's my new email address?"

Luca wasn't surprised that it seemed totally unfamiliar. The name seemed cute but unreal: DearDear. She didn't recognize the company name that appeared after the "at" symbol, but that was fine as long as it worked.

"Is it okay if I send a trial email to you to make sure it works?" she asked Scott.

He was fine with that. His email address made sense since it contained a Sherridan at the beginning and a well-known domain name company at the end. "This isn't the address I usually use, but I give it out to get information or even spam from people I don't want contacting me most of the time. Since you're here, you won't be emailing me much, so I'm giving you this one. When you leave sometime in the future, I'll make sure you have my real address."

Leave. Sometime in the future. A shudder went through Luca. Yes, she wanted to leave sometime with Nicky, especially so her son could have a real life.

But not for a while, not until she could be sure he was safe. Her too.

A wonderment shot through her then. The staff members here at the shelter might be here forever, but she understood they were kept safe, protected for a while, and then the idea was that a new home would be found for them in a location far different from where they'd been before, still using their new identity.

That was what she wished for Nicky and herself. But she wondered if Mark would still be here then, or whether he'd be relocated long before them.

If so, though she only just met him, she knew she'd miss him.

And she figured that former staff members weren't supposed to get back in touch with one another.

Maybe she could ask Mark in an appropriate way how long he anticipated being at the shelter. She'd have to figure out how.

For the moment, she had an email to send.

Even so, she couldn't help thinking about her son. "Is there some way of confirming that Nicky's okay now?"

"If he weren't, I'm sure we'd hear about it. Someone would have rushed up here to find us and let us know."

Scott's smile was sweet, Luca thought. He seemed to care about her, and her concern about her son.

Well, to have a job like he did, he must really give a damn about people in general, and the ones he helped in particular.

"Got it," she said. "I'll go ahead and send you the sample email. And—well, how do I get Mitzi's? Will you send it to me?"

"Exactly," Scott said. "But first, go ahead and use the account that's already open on the computer—your new email address. Send me that sample email to the address I just told you."

She did. In moments, Scott, using his phone, replied and sent her the email address she was supposed to use for Mitzi.

All seemed well.

"I just got a text that I have to follow up on, so I'm returning to my office. Go ahead and email Mitzi, but let me know if you have any problems. And come to my office to tell me when you're heading back downstairs. In the meantime, I'll let you know if I hear anything about Nicky, but I'm sure all's fine."

"Great. Thank you."

Luca watched as Scott exited the office and closed the door behind him. She felt mixed emotions. She was alone for the moment, with no protector, and that hadn't happened since Nicky and she had arrived early that morning.

But she was still in the shelter. Scott was down the hall. There might be other managers nearby in other offices.

And Mark? Well, he was somewhere at the shelter. He would protect the staff members, she was sure, even as he was being protected. He certainly gave the impression of wanting to shield those in need—like her and her son.

Enough of that. She was sitting on this stiff chair and leaned toward the laptop computer in front of her.

She copied Mitzi's address from Scott's email, then pasted it into the "To" line of a fresh email.

Hi, Mitzi, she typed. This is Luca. I'm fine and I hope you are too. I've relocated with Nicky to a really good place and appreciate you letting me know about it. Stay well.

Then she sent it. Would that be enough? She hoped it started a conversation, but she wasn't sure when or if she'd be able to check on it. Well, she'd just request the ability to look again from Scott, although she figured Mitzi would probably let him know she'd heard from "Luca."

Okay. She'd done what she had come to do. Now it was time to go downstairs and make sure all was okay with Nicky.

But…

Okay. She knew it was a bad idea. She knew Scott had told her not to.

But who would know if she got into her regular email address to see if anything was there that she should know about?

As she'd considered before, it wasn't like a text message where someone could then learn where your phone was by using GPS.

She would be careful. No way would she do anything like respond to any messages that might have been sent to her old email address.

Was she just asking for trouble? Maybe.

But she had to look.

And she wasn't surprised when she logged into her

old email address to find a lot of spam, correspondence from some old friends, and quite a few ads for things for children: toys, clothes, books.

Or so she thought from the senders and headings.

She hadn't been gone from her home or her old computer long, but there was a lot of junk mail for just a couple of days.

She wasn't surprised, either, to see emails with addresses indicating they had come from the Cranstone police department.

Were George's former coworkers concerned about her?

Maybe. Though some had first names she didn't recognize. Others were clearly from Morley Boyle.

She should ignore them. She should sign off on this email address and get off the computer.

But she didn't. She opened one of the most recent emails from today that was clearly from Morley.

And gasped. Okay, she wasn't surprised. Morley indicated he'd sent her prior emails and was angry she hadn't responded.

It said:

You'd better respond now. Right now. I'm coming after you. And I have a good idea where you are.

But you can return home first, and if you do I'll be glad to see you and Davey—and in that case I won't hurt you.

Luca gasped.

He didn't say what he'd do if she didn't come back, but the indication was that he would harm her son and her.

Could he really find her here?

Had she made a major mistake checking her old email?

And why wasn't he worried that she would forward these to his superior officers?

He probably had a way to claim she'd sent them, not him.

Shaking, she logged out of that address. Maybe she should tell Scott after all.

But—she wouldn't do it immediately. She logged back into the address he'd given her.

Wow! Mitzi already responded.

How great to hear from you. Glad you're doing well. I'd like to keep in touch. And from all I know, you're in a good place. Don't come home anytime, now or in the future. And stay in touch as much as you can—this way. Things are not great around here. Take good care.

That, at least, she could mention to Scott.

What wasn't great around there? Something to do with Morley? Should she forward his emails to Mitzi? Maybe, but shouldn't Scott see them first?

For now, she'd try to ignore them while staying in touch with Mitzi, as she'd requested. Surely, Scott would let her do that.

Time to let him know about Mitzi's email and get out of there.

And to let him know she had disobeyed his order not to check her old email address? Maybe so, under these circumstances. For now, she'd think about it.

She couldn't wait to get back to Nicky. And…well, seeing Mark again might help her state of mind.

Assuming he was as kind and protective as he'd led her to believe so far.

Chapter 7

Sneaking back into the shelter was as challenging as sneaking out. Mark did what he had before with Rocky, striding along the street until they got to the park, checking around and avoiding other people as much as possible, hiding behind trees when he could and then walking slowly when there were no cars traveling the street.

In the shelter's parking lot, it was a bit easier since he could hide behind the few cars parked there with Rocky, then ease their way to the back of the wooden fence. He opened it quickly with his key card, slipped into the area behind the cafeteria building, then inside, where it was narrow and, fortunately, empty as usual.

Mark managed to take a deep, calming breath and praise his dog. "Good dog, Rocky," he said as he led the way up the stairs and into the area at the rear of the kitchen after changing his shirt.

All was well. And it wasn't dinnertime yet, so the place was, also fortunately, empty.

It was easy to slip out of there. In case anyone saw him, though, he grabbed a bottle of water from the refrigerator, which would be his excuse for entering the kitchen in the first place.

Okay, now what? He figured Rocky and he would do what staff members usually did this time of day— well, most of the day and not just nearing the dinner hour—and visit some of the animals under protection. That always meant hanging out with other staffers under protection too.

Like Luca and her little Nicky? Well, he certainly wouldn't mind seeing them.

He wasn't sure where he might find them now. Had Luca taken her son up to their apartment for a nap? Or had she continued to enjoy watching Nicky interact with the dogs he seemed to love to play with and possibly learn to train?

Whatever. "Hey, Rocky," he said as they entered the central area from the cafeteria where Mark noticed that, unsurprisingly, some staffers who helped prepare meals, like Sara, were just coming in to get started. "Let's go for a walk, shall we?"

Fortunately, the Doberman always seemed to enjoy walks. While within the facility it would involve less room and energy, Mark had no doubt Rocky would have fun even after their much longer walks outside the walls. Walks where, fortunately, no one had paid much attention to them.

Sara waved right away, and he waved back, smiling. He'd noticed earlier that her shelter shirt was a bright red. "Hey, good to see you here," he called. "I'm getting hungry." Not particularly true, but he figured he would enjoy dinner anyway.

"Give me a few," she yelled back. "And looks like I'm getting some help."

Sure enough, Denise, in a blue Chance Animal Shelter shirt, came into the cafeteria across from where Mark now walked with Rocky. "You definitely are," she said.

"Great! I'm definitely looking forward to dinner."

He wanted to walk around the shelter first. Maybe help with a little dog training. He'd done that before, and let other staffers work a bit with Rocky, though he didn't need the kind of training done here. But it never hurt to keep him in practice.

As he and his dog started down the walkway, not quite at the first dog-sheltering building, he looked around. Toward the side of that building, he saw Kathy working with Mocha and Leonard working with Jack, not surprised that they both were giving lessons together. There were often more staffers doing the same thing in the same place, although it appeared that, today, other groups of trainers were at other locations. That was a major idea around here: to keep those under protection active.

And little Nicky was there watching Leonard and Kathy.

Luca had to be there too. He began walking that way only to be stopped as Rocky pulled sideways on his leash, as if heading toward someone or something interesting.

That, it turned out, he was. Luca was right there. Mark gathered she'd come from near where he'd been, the main eating building. Or the office building. Maybe she'd had a meeting with Scott or one of the managers as another step in her becoming a staff member.

Only…well, he was speculating too much. She stopped to pat Rocky's head as the dog snuggled against her. Why was he being so pushy against her? That wasn't like his good boy.

As Mark regarded them, he saw something that made him want to give Luca a hug too. Though she seemed to be attempting to smile at his dog, he saw tears in her eyes.

What was wrong? He wanted to find out.

He edged over to her, rubbing Rocky's side and aiming a smile at Luca. "He's happy to see you," he said to begin their conversation. And Mark was happy to see her, too, he realized. Except that he was very concerned about what was on her mind.

Something about Nicky? The kid appeared to be having fun with the dogs and people near him. Although, if Mark was right, he looked a little tired.

And Luca? She appeared distressed. Sad? Angry? He couldn't tell what was causing those tears. Not yet.

But he would find out.

"I'm happy to see him too," she managed to say, her voice somewhat hoarse.

He kept his tone low even though no one was near them. "He's concerned that you seem upset. Can you tell him why?" And me, too, of course.

"I—I—" She'd been looking at Rocky but now she aimed her gaze totally at the ground as her eyes welled up even more.

"Hey," Mark said. "Let's go somewhere a bit more quiet, okay?"

It wasn't that noisy here, but additional privacy would be a good thing. He didn't wait for her reply, gently taking her arm and leading her back toward the main buildings. There weren't many isolated areas there, but he figured not many people would show up at the side of the office building, unless a manager had something to do outside.

She didn't object, but walked with him, still apparently more interested in Rocky than anyone else for the moment. She even kept a hand on the dog's leash that Mark held the end of.

Soon, they stood in the shadows off to the side of the office building. Mark looked around. Nowhere to sit or to relax. He figured whatever they would talk about wouldn't be relaxing anyway.

"So tell me…" he finally said, unsuccessfully attempting to put his face in a position where she'd have to meet his eyes. "Something seems to be wrong. Please tell me about it, and I'll see what I can do to help."

He hoped it wasn't anything like she'd learned something bad about Nicky's health, or that for some reason the two of them would be kicked out of the shelter.

He wouldn't be able to do anything about either.

"I-I don't think I'm supposed to talk about it."

He did manage to bend over enough to see into her face. Or maybe she'd decided to at least look at him.

Yes, she was still one attractive woman, even with the dampness in her lovely hazel eyes and the sorrow he saw marring the rest of her pretty face. The slight breeze helped her light blue Chance Animal Shelter T-shirt hug her body a bit, enhancing its already enticing curves.

But he shouldn't be noticing that.

"Maybe not," he said. "And we don't know each other well. Not yet, at least. But you saw me before in my cowboy hat. I've got lots of dependability and honor like the cowboy I used to be while growing up in Texas. I promise I won't tell anyone what you say."

He hoped that was right. It would certainly be his intention. But if the only way he could help her was to talk to someone—and he reckoned around here that would be Scott—he'd find a way to do it so that nothing came back to bite her.

Or he would at least do all he could to prevent it.

"Right," she said in a tone that suggested she didn't believe a word he said. Still, she continued. "I need to trust someone. I trust Scott, but he won't trust me since I did something he told me not to do. But there was good reason. An even better reason than I figured, once I did it and learned what I did."

Sounded puzzling, but hopefully he would understand once she explained, and he assumed she would explain something considering what she'd said. "Yes," he said, "you can definitely trust me."

"Well… Scott allowed me to use the internet. He

gave me a new email address because the person who'd helped me before, who'd told me about this shelter so I could escape here with Nicky, was trying to get in touch with me by way of Scott. He said I should only contact her once with the new email address, which I did, and not tell any of the staff members that I was allowed to send an email."

She looked at him as if attempting to determine what he thought about her misdeed of breaching that instruction.

He only nodded, without saying anything to indicate he was upset that he hadn't been given the same privilege.

Well, heck. She didn't know that he even had a phone. And more. Or that he was there undercover, attempting to help her and the other staff members. He was obeying the rules, at least for now, keeping that quiet.

Since he didn't react, she went on. "That person got back to me when I said Nicky and I were where she'd suggested and doing well. She let me know she was glad to hear that."

Luca actually smiled then, and it lit up her face so much that the beauty he'd seen there before appeared amplified. He smiled back. "I can understand that," he said, though he had an inkling of what she might have done to make Scott mad.

Had she contacted someone else she wasn't supposed to?

"I let Scott know about our email correspondence, as he'd told me to do. But—"

Ah. That *but* was probably about what she'd done that was a no-go.

"But what?" he urged gently.

"But…well, I also did what he'd told me not to. I checked my old email address. I figured I wouldn't respond to anything, and it wasn't like I was making a call on a phone where someone could track down where I was. And I didn't send any emails using that address."

Her tone had changed in a way he interpreted as hoping for his understanding.

Not that he necessarily agreed with her disobeying Scott, but he hadn't heard anything too bad. Not yet, at least.

He reached down to pat Rocky since the dog seemed to be straining slightly at his leash. At the calming touch Rocky sat and looked up at Mark, who nodded at him. "Good boy," he said and then looked back up at Luca. "I understand."

He sort of did. He did understand how difficult it must be for real staff members to be stuck here, yes, under protective custody, but unable to contact even those friends and family members who weren't endangering them.

Even by trading emails.

Luca smiled slightly and looked down at Rocky too. "Well, right or wrong, I did it, and I haven't admitted it to Scott. I don't want to get myself in trouble with him, especially now. And maybe I'd be better off not knowing what I now know. I wouldn't be so worried if it wasn't for Nicky. But my son— Well, I don't think we're totally in danger now, but still…"

"What is it?" Mark tried to keep his voice soft and encouraging, but her words worried him. Not *totally* in danger?

She considered them at least somewhat endangered, even in this place, at this time?

"It's the man who attempted to seduce me after my husband was murdered. The guy I now suspect as being the murderer." Her voice cracked as she continued to look down at the now placid dog.

Mark felt anything but placid. He knew where this might be going.

Did the guy know where Luca and her son were? Was he coming after them?

It turned out he was partly correct. Or, at least, that the guy still wanted to come after them.

"Tell me," he said as gently as he could.

"Morley sent me a lot of emails in the short time I was gone. He fortunately doesn't seem to know where we are—at least not yet. But he demanded that I come home with Nicky right away. He said he'd find me anyway. And I'm afraid he'll hurt us too."

She could well be right, Mark knew, especially if the guy had killed her husband.

And if she hadn't seen those emails, would things be any different? The guy sounded like a dangerous nutcase, apparently not even worried those emails would be seen by others.

The fact that Luca had seen them didn't necessarily help her. She wasn't going anywhere, and hanging out here still seemed the best thing for her and her son. Or, at least, that was what Mark believed.

But he might well renege on his promise to keep what she said quiet.

He would need to discuss it with Scott.

Maybe, with their respective cop connections, they could learn more about this guy and bring him down before he could make good on any of his threats.

Though that hadn't happened before. And far as Mark recalled, the guy remained a cop on the force where he'd worked with Luca's husband.

Somehow Luca seemed to read his mind. "You're going to talk to Scott about this, aren't you?"

"Only if I can't figure out any other way to protect you and Nicky," he said.

Instead of shouting at him or slugging him, she threw her arms around him in a wonderful but unanticipated hug.

"Thank you for wanting to protect us," she said softly. And then, even more surprisingly, she gave him a quick but warm kiss.

Chapter 8

"Mommy!"

Luca was suddenly awakened by her son's voice. He was shaking her arm as she lay on her new bed under the sheets and blanket provided, in their new apartment in their new location.

The Chance Animal Shelter. They had now spent a night here.

Under protection.

She quickly turned sideways to glance at Nicky. "Good morning, sweetheart," she said, looking into her son's face, almost at her level as she continued to lie there. He appeared concerned, his brown eyes huge, his mouth in a pout. "Is everything okay?"

"It's morning. And…and I don't know where we are."

Luca smiled. "This is our new home, Nicky. Remember? We came here to this very special place yesterday, and we met lots of nice people, and doggies too. And this is now our own apartment." She sat up, slipped out of bed and knelt on the floor, hugging him. He was warm, and he hugged her back. "You were pretty sleepy when we came up here last night and got your bath, so I'm not surprised you don't remember it all. But we're going to be here for now, and we'll have a lot of fun."

She hoped. But she would certainly do all she could to ensure Nicky had the best experience possible here.

They definitely had people on their side, including Director Scott…and Mark.

"Let's get dressed, okay? Then we'll go downstairs and have breakfast in that nice cafeteria where we ate yesterday."

"Okay, Mommy."

Luca quickly walked him down the hall to the small bedroom that contained the other bed, where she had tucked him in last night.

She then had gone back into her living room, where Mark had brought Scott so they could talk.

As she helped her son dress, she couldn't help remembering that difficult yet helpful conversation. It had remained on her mind, kept her awake somewhat, yet it also had allowed her to relax and finally fall asleep.

Oh, yes, she had done the right thing by moving here.

With these wonderful people who would take care of them.

Especially Mark. He could have listened to her, and avoided telling their director about what she had done.

But she realized it had been totally appropriate for

Mark to tell Scott, who, despite scolding her briefly for disobeying him, focused instead on the terrible emails she had seen and what they would do about it.

Not just her, but *they*.

"Am I wearing my new shirt again today, Mommy?"

"Yes, honey. I'll have to see if we can get extra shirts so we can wash them and still have another one to wear that has the name of this special place on it."

Nicky already put his hands up and she pulled the shirt down over them. He peered at her. "What's the name?" he asked.

She'd mentioned it a few times before but wasn't surprised he didn't remember. "The Chance Animal Shelter," she said.

He looked at her. "You're still in your PJs. Will you wear your—" he grinned at her as he continued "—Chance Animal Shelter shirt today?"

"I certainly will," she said with a laugh. Gladly so.

And, hopefully, it would be warm enough outside that neither of them would need to wear a jacket.

She wondered what would happen today. Maybe it had already begun. During the brief discussion here in the apartment with Mark and Scott last night, she'd apologized for checking the emails with her old address despite Scott's warning her not to. He'd acted okay with it despite admonishing her to listen to what he said in the future.

Under the circumstances, he indicated that maybe it was a good thing she'd ignored him this one time, but she needed to understand that the rules here were strict, and she had better not do it again. He said he would notify Morley's superiors at the Cranstone PD after a discussion with Officer Mitzi Rhodes regarding who could be trusted.

Luca also gave them the password for her email address so Scott and Mark could check it. And both told her not to use one of the shelter's computers or access it herself again until she'd gotten their okay.

She didn't object to that. Nor did she make any promises and, fortunately, they didn't ask any of her. But her curiosity, and even more her concern, would most likely cause her to check it now and then to see what, if anything, Morley had added.

Or if they'd deleted everything of his, which she sort of hoped would be the case.

Still, she recognized that as protectors, they did need to see what was there. And she hoped never to see what was there, or anything else from Morley, ever again—although she figured he'd likely send more.

Now, once she helped Nicky into his outfit including his red shelter T-shirt, she gave him a coloring book and crayons to work on a picture while she dressed. But her mind hadn't stopped its churning around the issues in her life. Hers and Nicky's.

Yes, he was occupied for the moment. But coloring wasn't enough for her son. More and more, even when she'd woken up last night now and then, she'd been worrying about the fact she'd had to take Nicky out of preschool. She needed materials to help him prepare to attend school again…someday. And somewhere. Hopefully no later than next fall, when he could start kindergarten.

She'd already created a bit of a disturbance here. Would it be another one if she asked Scott if she could go online or in person to buy some educational items for her son?

Even if it was, she had to do it.

Nicky and she were ready to leave. "Let's go to breakfast, okay?" she said after she returned to his bedroom.

"Okay, Mommy."

She locked the apartment door behind them after they stepped into the hallway and considered walking down the stairs with him, but not yet. She led him to the elevator.

The car stopped on the third floor as it descended and Kathy got on it. Her Chance Animal Shelter T-shirt today was navy blue, a darker shade than Luca's light blue. Even though the older woman did great while training energetic dogs, maybe avoiding steps helped her keep her own energy too.

In any case, Luca was glad to see her. So was Nicky.

"Good morning!" he exclaimed. "Can we work with doggies today again?"

"Good morning." Kathy grinned at the boy. "I'll be working with them, and if it's okay with your mommy, you can too." She looked at Luca.

"Of course," she said. "But let's have breakfast first."

"That's certainly my intention."

They soon reached the bottom floor and exited, Luca holding Nicky's hand. Other staff members were in the downstairs lobby, heading for the cafeteria, and all three of them did the same.

Once inside, Luca looked around. The place unsurprisingly appeared as it had yesterday, with food tables at the end and long tables for seating along the way, with a few seats occupied.

She couldn't help glancing around to see if Mark was there, even though the person she needed to talk to yet again was Scott. As it turned out, both were in the line waiting to get food, with Rocky beside Mark on the floor. And so Luca aimed Nicky in that direction, saying hi to staff members along the way who'd already sat at tables.

Their place in line was several people behind Scott and Mark, but before settling in to wait, Luca edged up to them to say good morning. She had an urge to ask Mark to save them seats but didn't have to. He didn't tell her to butt in line, but said, "See you at the table where we sat at dinner last night, okay?"

"Sounds good." And it did. She returned to the line where she'd told Nicky stay, and watched as those in front of them chose their breakfasts. It looked like good stuff, scrambled eggs, toast, cereal and more, all things that Nicky liked. And her too.

It wasn't long before she was able to pick up paper plates and have Nicky tell her what he wanted. She needed to get a bowl for him, too, since he was in the mood for cereal—a kind without a lot of sugar, fortunately. She chose eggs and toast.

As they finished collecting their meals, she looked around. Sure enough, Mark sat at the same table where they'd been yesterday, near the door. There were empty seats beside him. She carried her plate and Nicky's bowl perched on another plate, and they headed that way.

She put the plates on the table. "Okay if we sit here?"

"Definitely."

Near him was Kathy, who'd gotten ahead of them in line, plus Bibi and Leonard. Today, he'd tied Rocky to the back of his chair, and the dog lay on the floor beside him. The dog looked up and wagged his tail as Nicky bent to pat him before Luca told him to take a seat.

Luca settled Nicky onto a chair beside Mark, leaving the one on Nicky's other side empty for her. Her son looked up questioningly. "I'm going to get your milk now," she told him. And some coffee for herself. "Anybody need anything?"

She looked at the others, who mostly shook their heads and said, "No thanks." When she caught Mark's eyes, he also shook his head, but there was something in his expression that suggested he did need something. Maybe something he wouldn't put into words.

Something similar to the heat that flashed through her, which she ignored.

"I'll be right back," she said, looking at Nicky. No sense making what she said sound suggestive, since it wasn't.

But she wondered what it was about that man that made him so attractive to her. Well, she certainly would not pursue it.

For now, she hurried to the back of the room again. It was becoming more crowded but she made it to the drink table fairly quickly and was glad to see Scott was there, talking with Nella and Denise. She said her hellos and smiled at all of them, but then she neared Scott to ask if they could talk.

He walked away with her for a few steps and looked at her questioningly. "About…what's going on?"

"Yes," she said. "And more. I need your opinion about how I can get some adequate educational materials that I can use to teach Nicky since… I assume I won't be able to get him into preschool for a while, if ever. And he needs to be prepared for when I find a way to get him into real school when he's older."

"Got it." He looked at his watch then back at her. "Come up to my office in about an hour and we'll talk about it."

"Sounds good." She smiled again then went to the table to pick up a glass of milk for Nicky, which she could also pour into his cereal, and a cup of coffee for herself.

It looked like she might be talking a lot with the director as long as she stayed here, which was fine with her—as long as it always led to good things for her son too.

She returned to the table, where she got Nicky's cereal ready for him to eat, and then sat down. Nicky started spooning out his flakes, and Luca looked at Mark beside her. "Thanks for saving us seats."

"Anytime." He smiled. She noticed he had chosen pretty much the same breakfast as her, only a larger quantity of eggs and an extra piece of toast.

"What are you up to today?" she asked as she began eating. Probably the same kinds of things she would be doing with Nicky, she presumed—caring for shelter dogs, maybe walking them inside the central area, and perhaps allowing Nicky to be instructed more by those who trained the dogs.

"Not much," he said. "Not much I can do to help with your outside email stuff, after all." He kept his voice low so no one else could hear.

She felt herself flush. "No, but I appreciate your concern. And…well, I'll be talking to Scott about some things soon, and I'm sure we'll discuss it at least a bit more then."

"I'm sure you will," he said. He took a sip of coffee as he looked at her. His blue eyes appeared angry at first, though she realized he wasn't angry with her. But then they softened. "Scott will figure out a way to make sure you remain safe here. No question about that."

"Of course." She could only hope for now that it was true.

Mark enjoyed eating breakfast here, as always, and especially so considering the current company at his table.

He hoped Luca and Nicky would hang out with him for meals for as long as they were here. As long as he was here.

But the timing for both couldn't yet be predicted. And whatever happened, he wanted to ensure that the lovely lady who smiled as she sat at his side and ate and talked to the other staffers around them as well as her son, remained okay and hopefully found a nice, secure and highly safe new home somewhere, sometime soon. He doubted it would be a good thing for them to hang out in the facility for long. If nothing else, the kid needed to grow up somewhere where he could have an actual life, not a protective shelter forever.

That would be better for his mama too. Although whenever and wherever that was, Mark realized he was unlikely to see them again. That wasn't something he was eager for, even after knowing them for such a short time.

But they needed to be somewhere else, with that guy threatening them out of their lives forever.

And, eventually, Mark's assignment here would be over. Even now, he wondered how long it would continue. At the moment, the reason he'd been sent here, to watch the residents and report on their outside contacts, didn't seem too useful.

He hadn't discovered outside contacts, and the police where he actually worked hadn't seemed to learn anything new either. Maybe it had just been some kind of rumor or misunderstanding that had meant nothing. He would continue checking it out, just in case.

He took a long sip of coffee. It was getting cold. He needed to leave the cafeteria and go talk to Scott briefly.

He figured he'd head downtown to the police station again today, even though he'd just been there.

But they needed to make sure the local PD got in touch with the cops in the department where Luca's husband had worked, and where that snake Morley still worked. They needed to know what the guy was doing, and how to end his email threats to Luca.

And to determine if they were a further indication of his guilt in what had happened to her husband.

"So what are you up to today?" Luca asked. Had she

been reading his mind, recognizing he was pondering exactly that—what he would be doing soon?

"I have a few things in mind." Like having his discussion with Scott and heading downtown with Rocky. But he wouldn't tell her that.

"Any chance you could work with Nicky and show him how you teach Rocky his commands, maybe take them for a walk?"

He knew she meant inside the enclosure of the shelter. He'd be taking his K-9 for a walk, but outside, and without their company.

"Unfortunately, I've got some stuff I need to read in my apartment, so I don't think I'll have time today, but we can do it soon, I hope."

"Okay," she said, her tone perky, her expression a bit sad. He would have loved to continue the conversation but didn't think it was a good idea.

And what could he claim he was reading in his apartment that would be more important than hanging around outside with Luca and Nicky—and Rocky, of course?

He noticed Scott a couple tables over, now saying his goodbyes, wishing the staffers around him a good day. He was heading for his office.

That meant Mark needed to go there too. But he didn't need anyone else to know.

He waited a short while, talking to those around him. Talking to Nicky a bit and encouraging him to work with some dogs today.

"Will you be there?" The little boy's voice sounded eager.

Mark almost wished he could say yes. Instead, he

told Nicky, "Not at first. But I'm going to try to work things out for later today so we can help Rocky with his commands, then maybe try them with other dogs too. Okay?"

"Okay!"

Mark knew he had to work that out somehow. Especially when he looked into Luca's eyes as she regarded him above her son's head. She looked dubious. But did he see a little hope there?

"Okay," he said again, this time nodding toward Luca as he stood. Rocky rose, too, and waited for Mark to use his leash to direct him.

Mark quickly moved toward the door then, once outside, walked around the compound just a little so he could head upstairs to Scott's office without being too obvious about it.

Once they reached the top floor, Mark knocked on Scott's door and immediately heard, "Come in."

He did, Rocky in front of him. Scott sat behind his desk, looking at him. "So what are you doing here?" he asked. "I figured you knew you needed to sneak a walk downtown and coordinate with the Chance and Cranstone PDs about checking into that Morley and those damned emails."

Mark grinned and gave a brief salute. "On it right away."

Chapter 9

Luca couldn't help wondering what Mark was up to that morning. But it didn't matter. The staff members around them were interacting with Nicky, asking him if he wanted to work with doggies right now.

Unsurprisingly, that was exactly what her son wanted to do.

She loved the idea. But first she needed to talk with Scott. Although, if yesterday was a good example, she could go with Kathy and Chessie and the others, watch them start working with Nicky and some of the dogs, then leave her son to be minded by these wonderful, caring folks who were also under protection.

For now, she waited, taking another sip of her cooling coffee while Nicky finished drinking his glass of milk. When he was done, they both rose and bussed their dishes to the table designated for that. Nicky knew the drill now and carried his paper plate, bowl and spoon, and Luca, carrying his empty glass along with her things, cheered him on.

In a minute, they headed for the door, where Kathy waited for them. She knelt to Nicky's level. "Want to work with Mocha again today? I think he's doing really well, and if he does a good job today, you and I can push Mr. Scott to work harder on finding him a forever home, okay?"

Her smart son nodded eagerly, but then his expression sobered. "But we'll miss him if he goes away."

Kathy nodded and gave Nicky a hug. "Yes, we will. But we'll know we've done a really good job training him. He'll be happy in a home of his own with other people who love him. And we can work with other pups here who also need forever homes. Will you help me with that?"

"Yes!" Nicky said vehemently.

Then, looking at Luca first, Kathy took Nicky's hand. "Let's go get Mocha."

After Luca saw what a great job they were doing again with the terrier mix, and Chessie joined them with Oodles, the poodle mix who had apparently only recently been brought to the shelter, Luca said, "Is it okay if I leave Nicky with you two for a few minutes?" She didn't tell them she needed to talk with Scott. They didn't have to know what she'd be up to, although they might recognize where she was headed.

"Of course!" Pretty Chessie aimed a big smile that lit up her green eyes toward Luca, which made her smile back.

It would be better this way. Some of the things she wanted to ask Scott shouldn't be said in Nicky's presence.

She got a glimpse of Mark and Rocky heading away from the apartment building—or the office building? They seemed a bit closer to that structure. And where were they heading? She considered going after them to see why Mark was out of his apartment. He'd said he would be reading there for most of the day, at least until late afternoon when they could get together again.

But she wasn't particularly close to that end of the shelter. Maybe he'd just taken Rocky outside and would go up a back stairway to return to their apartment, since she didn't see them again.

She could ask Mark about it later. Would he tell her where he'd gone? Why not? It wasn't as if a staff member and his dog could go very far on the shelter grounds.

Right now, she needed to speak to Scott, while others she trusted, at least sort of, were watching Nicky.

A few other staff members were exercising dogs along the center path not far from where she stood. Nothing surprising there. She wasn't about to ask any of them if they happened to have seen Mark.

Instead, she turned to her side and looked over to where Nicky hung out with Kathy and Chessie, saw him raise his hand and lower it, finger pointed, as if giving one of the dogs a command. Luca smiled. Her son seemed fine.

And so she headed for the office building.

She decided to walk up the stairs. She needed more daily exercise than the little she'd gotten since they'd arrived and needed to plan for it. She would have to do more stair-walking and extra things. She needed to ask about what others did in addition to walking dogs.

But right now, she needed to meet with Scott.

He invited her in as soon as she knocked on his door. Could he have known it was her, thanks to the security cameras, or would he just assume it was her because they'd briefly discussed her coming to see him when they were at breakfast?

"Hi, Luca," he said as she entered, not rising from behind his desk.

Okay, it didn't matter if he'd known it was her or not. What mattered was how they'd hold their conversation, and what it would contain.

"Hi, Scott. I appreciate the opportunity for us to talk again, and I hope you're not too mad at me for not obeying what you told me with the emails."

"Like I said," he said dryly, "under the circumstances, it was a good thing you checked your old email address. But as I also said, don't do it any more on your own, although you can ask me to give you computer access and consent if you want to look again."

"Got it," she said, sitting in one of the chairs across from him without relaxing. She did get that he'd backed off a bit, apparently relenting somewhat out of concern for her, which she appreciated.

Would she do as he told her from now on? She'd just have to see how things worked out. After all, how could anyone outside know if she'd accessed her former email address if she didn't respond to anything?

"So you wanted to talk about Nicky and how to prepare him for further education, right?"

"That's right. I had him in preschool for a while before, but now…"

"Too bad we don't have any teachers here as staff members, although I'm not aware of any who need witness protection." He shrugged slightly and raised his eyebrows.

Luca thought his jesting was somewhat cute under the circumstances. "Neither do I, unfortunately. Or fortunately for them. And I assume I can't access a way to get my son an online tutor to provide virtual classes." That kind of teacher wouldn't necessarily know where the student lived, but it might be possible to find out.

Not that Morley would know such a thing was occurring. But she believed someone as mentally deranged and determined as he seemed to be, and with his cop background, might already be attempting any number of routes to find them, so she couldn't be certain they'd stay under the radar.

"That's very true," Scott confirmed. "But I've thought about it a bit and have an idea. Nicky could be our experiment in this as well as simply being here. I've checked online and there are some very basic, toy-like computers to teach young kids the alphabet and how to spell and read some words, even learn their own names. Plus, there are some smartphone kinds of gadgets that help teach kids numbers and basic arithmetic, as well as learn to sing along with kiddy songs. I'll show them to you online and order a couple if you think they'll be good for Nicky. I'll have them delivered elsewhere, of course, but they should end up here soon."

"Really? That sounds wonderful!" Luca knew she sounded excited. "But…well, I wish I could offer to pay for them, but as you know my resources are limited. I could work out repaying you in installments, making a deposit now, but I'm not sure how I'll be able to earn any income for a while."

"Exactly." Scott shook his head but looked at her as if he appreciated what she'd said. "No income. No deposit. You're under our protection in a lot of ways, and that includes financially. Fortunately, we have some good donors. We'll hang on to the gadgets here at the shelter. Nicky will be able to use them as much as he likes. And, although we hope we'll find you somewhere else to go before he misses too much real school, even kindergarten, we can acquire more sophisticated stuff for him, if you're here for a while and he needs it for his learning."

Luca made herself smile at that. She was definitely happy to hear they would work with her and her son as long as they needed protection. But she really didn't want them to stay beyond a few months—as long as it was safe for them to leave.

"So, don't worry about not paying," Scott continued. "The learning tools will remain ours, and we'll make them available for others in the future. If we get more kids here while you and Nicky are still around, we'll see how Nicky does with what we acquire and buy duplicates of the good items for any other children."

"Thank you," Luca said, hoping she sounded as appreciative as she felt. She wasn't about to tell Scott about her hopes of leaving soon.

She knew some staff members had been at the shelter for a long time. But they didn't have kids here who needed a real life.

Luca moved on to her next topic. "In the mean-time…"

She didn't have to say any more.

"I assume you want to know what we're doing to protect the two of you. How we're looking into your buddy, Morley, and the emails he sent you, and how we can repress any further possibilities he has of finding, and hurting, you. One thing would be to talk to the right people about obtaining evidence that he killed your husband, assuming that was the case."

Luca half rose, wanting to shout something about it definitely being the case, but to what avail?

She could say so by shouting, or otherwise, and that still wouldn't get Morley arrested. He remained a cop, after all, as far as she knew. His coworkers and superiors apparently hadn't chosen to connect him with George's murder. Or if they had, they hadn't followed up to arrest him.

Yet how could she make it "otherwise" from here?

How could she make it "otherwise" even if she wasn't here? At least this way, Morley couldn't find her—or Nicky.

She forced herself to sit back down again. "That's right," she said quietly. "I'd appreciate hearing about whatever you've done, whoever you've told about the situation, and whether anyone will be following up, trying to bring Morley to justice—and keep him from threatening me."

"Or worse, finding you," Scott added. "Oh, yes. I've got things in the works, people I've already notified and others who are assisting outside the shelter in determining the real situation and ensuring that Morley doesn't find you, and is taken into custody once some proof is found of what he did."

"Assuming anyone else really believes he did it," Luca murmured, looking down at her lap.

"That's one of the multiple reasons to find some evidence," Scott said, nodding. "And for now, I'm putting feelers out there with contacts I've got, asking them to look into it. Fast and deep."

"Thank you," Luca said, even more vehemently than before. "I can't begin to tell you how much I appreciate what you're doing." She just hoped he and his contacts got some results—soon.

"You just did," Scott said. "Again. Now, tell you what. We'll get on my computer together here and see what kinds of educational fun things we can find for Nicky."

"Oh, yes." Luca's gratitude was overwhelming. "I... I'd love to help in the process. But I can't stay too long since I have to go save the staffers who're helping out with my son." She laughed along with Scott.

She didn't mention that she had someone else she hoped to meet with sometime that afternoon.

Nor did she mention she'd seen then lost sight of Mark a short while ago.

But she couldn't help wondering how he'd slipped around the buildings, and where he'd gone.

Finally. Rocky and Mark were near downtown Chance. Striding briskly but carefully.

Leaving the shelter for a walk—and police department visit—was as challenging as it always was.

Maybe more so this time since Mark had seen Luca heading in his direction just before he'd left the shelter and had wondered if she was going to hurry over and say hi, delaying and hindering his departure.

Fortunately, she hadn't. He'd been able to slip around the corner of the building.

He'd done his now normal routine of looking around to make sure no one was watching and then slipping through the cafeteria, changing his shirt, and heading outside. Using his key card to open the fence gate. Cautiously observing the somewhat busy park, moving along the street a bit until he felt comfortable crossing, then walking with Rocky through the park. And downtown to the civic center, heading for the police station.

Now inside, he led Rocky up the back stairs to the third floor.

He'd called Assistant Chief Kara during his walk, and she promised to have Chief Shermovski drop in while they were talking. "He's the one who's been in most contact with the people at the Cranstone PD, after all," she'd told him.

Then he was definitely the one Mark wanted to talk to, although he knew Kara had spoken a couple of times with Scott about the situation and the recent emailed threats from Morley to Luca. She knew a lot about what had gone on. But now it was most important to know who was doing something about it—and what they were doing.

As he walked up the stairs with Rocky, he saw a couple other officers he knew and they greeted one another without questioning him why he was out of uniform.

Even though they didn't know he was undercover elsewhere, they knew better than to discuss his appearance here or his assignment. They did say hi to Rocky and some gave him a pat.

Once more, he entered Kara's office, this time with a brief knock before opening her door. Unsurprisingly, she said, "Come in." He was already inside and seated in a chair, Rocky down at his feet, by the time she finished.

"Okay," she said. "Good to see you. And I think we'll have an interesting discussion today. Sherm will join us soon. He's already told me a bit about what he's learned."

That tantalized Mark's mind. His visit here would be productive. He'd hopefully leave with more knowledge about what was happening, maybe even about what he could do to help and who else he could contact— although he'd have to be particularly cautious with his efforts.

They had to wait for Sherm. How long? He had an urge to prod Kara, gently of course, but hopefully get her talking—

"I can see those wheels turning in your head." She leaned over her desk, arms crossed on its top, her brown eyes almost glaring. She looked comfortable in the white shirt of her uniform that contrasted nicely with her short black hair. They mostly got along well together, and Mark didn't want to blow that now.

"Yeah, I could be overthinking this, but I don't think so. Even though watching over that new staff member at the shelter, now called Luca, isn't my job, I've come to want to help take care of all of those under protection at the facility. And yes, I know I'm supposed to be keeping an eye on them, trying to learn more about any outsiders who staffers inappropriately remain in contact with that might endanger the place. Which I'm doing. But since I haven't seen anything, and apparently you still haven't, either, I'm trying to continue doing my job by helping in whatever way I can. Like observing. And following up when there's an issue. Like—"

"Like those emails. I understand. And appreciate it. But don't overstep—"

She didn't get to finish since her door opened and the police chief strode in. That got Rocky's attention. He stood beside Mark's chair and began wagging his tail.

"Hi, guy." Sherm walked over to pat Rocky's head before he took a seat beside Mark, facing Kara's desk. "And hi to you, guy," he said to Mark, grinning enough that his facial wrinkles seemed to deepen. "Glad you came, though I know it's not easy to sneak away. But it's easier to fill you in on what I've learned here than wondering whether stuff I say on the phone to Scott and you is also being heard by others at your shelter. Even though, right now, we don't have any reason to mistrust anyone who's there, it's better to be as safe as possible."

"Agreed," Mark said, though he did wonder why things seemed so okay at the shelter with its staff members. Was this the calm before an upcoming storm?

Well, he hoped not, but that was why he was there.

"So here's the short rundown." Sherm leaned closer toward Mark. "I don't really know anyone at the Cranstone PD well, but I understood that one of the officers there, Mitzi Rhodes, was the one who referred the new staff member they now call Luca to the Chance Animal Shelter." He looked at Mark as if requesting his concurrence.

"That's what I understand," he agreed.

"Well, I contacted Mitzi—carefully, of course. Told her who I was, and a bit about the situation. I called the staff member in question by her real name—Cathleen—so Mitzi would be sure of who I was talking about."

Again he looked at Mark, who nodded.

"I told her a bit about what was going on, some threatening emails Cathleen had received, apparently from one of their officers—Morley Boyle. Asked which of the higher-ups there, preferably a chief or assistant chief, could be trusted for me to contact with this information and some questions. She gave me the name of Chief Rudy Rincoll. I thanked her and said I'd call him, so she might want to give him a heads-up. And I'd like to call him with you here, although I don't want you to say anything. Got it?"

"Absolutely."

"Can I listen in too?" Kara asked.

"Yep. We'll call right now."

Sherm pulled a phone from his pocket as well as a piece of paper that he looked at before pressing in some numbers. He held it to his ear without putting the speaker on.

Someone must have answered, and they had a short conversation in which Sherm identified himself: Chief Andrew Shermovski of the Chance PD. Apparently, the person he spoke with recognized the name.

"I'd like to put you on speaker so my assistant chief

and an officer working on the situation I'm calling about can listen, okay?"

Evidently it was, so Sherm pressed the button and Mark could hear the rest of the conversation.

It was brief. Sherm told Chief Rincoll, whom he introduced to Kara and Mark, about the email a former resident of Cranstone, who was now in protective custody—though he didn't specify where—had received from one of their officers, Morley Boyle. He offered to send Rincoll a copy.

Interesting. Scott must have forwarded it to Sherm.

The chief didn't have to offer specifics. Rincoll immediately said, "This is that situation with Cathleen Almera, widow of our officer George Almera, right?"

"Yes," Sherm said.

"She already accused Boyle of being the one to commit homicide on her husband rather than the suspect we had in custody, or so I heard. She didn't do anything official. And then she disappeared. Even if you sent something, I'd have a hard time believing it. Even so, though I sort of mentioned it to Boyle before, I'll talk to him further, watch and listen to how he reacts and see how things go. Then I'll call you back—on this number, right?"

"That's right," Sherm said, "although with the threat involved now—it might be better if you modified how you approach him."

"I'll be as discreet as I can."

They said their goodbyes and hung up.

Mark felt miserable. It didn't sound like anything

would be accomplished this way. He doubted that the other chief would be discreet.

And Luca might be threatened even more once Morley learned she'd ignored his command to keep quiet about it and his chief had heard of her accusations.

"Okay," Sherm said. "I'll let you know when I hear back from him."

If he did.

"Good," Mark replied. "I'll be eager to hear what he says." Not that he'd necessarily believe it. "But now, is there something else we should talk about, any rumors you've heard about staffers contacting anyone outside? If not, I think Rocky and I will head back to the shelter. I haven't gotten any info from or about staffers there about contacts like that, but I want to get back to listening, since that's what I'm there for."

"Go for it," Kara said. "And let's all keep in touch."

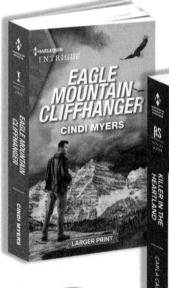

Get up to 4
FREE FABULOUS BOOKS
You Love!

To thank you for being a loyal reader we'd like to send you up to 4 FREE BOOKS, absolutely free when you try the Harlequin Reader Service.

Just write "YES" on the Loyal Reader Voucher and we'll send you 2 free books from each series you choose and Free Mystery Gifts, altogether worth over $20.

Try **Harlequin® Romantic Suspense** books featuring heart-racing page-turners with unexpected plot twists and irresistible chemistry that will keep you guessing to the very end.

Try **Harlequin Intrigue® Larger-Print** books featuring action-packed stories that will keep you on the edge of your seat. Solve the crime and deliver justice at all costs.

Or **TRY BOTH** and get 2 books from each series!

Your free books are completely free, even the shipping! If you continue with your subscription, you can look forward to curated monthly shipments of brand-new books from your selected series, always at a discount off the cover price! Plus you can cancel any time.

So don't miss out, return your Loyal Readers Voucher today to get your Free books.

Pam Powers

LOYAL READER
FREE BOOKS VOUCHER

YES! I Love Reading, please send me up to 4 FREE BOOKS and Free Mystery Gifts from the series I select.

Just write in "YES" on the dotted line below then return this card today and we'll send your free books & gifts asap!

➡ YES ⬅

Which do you prefer?

	Harlequin® **Romantic** **Suspense** 240/340 HDL GRS9		**Harlequin** **Intrigue®** **Larger-Print** 199/399 HDL GRS9		**BOTH** 240/340 & 199/399 HDL GRTL

FIRST NAME

LAST NAME

ADDRESS

APT.#

CITY

STATE/PROV.

ZIP/POSTAL CODE

EMAIL ☐ Please check this box if you would like to receive newsletters and promotional emails from Harlequin Enterprises ULC and its affiliates. You can unsubscribe anytime.

HI/HRS-622-LR LRV22

◆HARLEQUIN® Reader Service —Here's how it works:

Accepting your 2 free books and 2 free gifts (gifts valued at approximately $10.00 retail) places you under no obligation to buy anything. You may keep the books and gifts and return the shipping statement marked "cancel." If you do not cancel, approximately one month later we'll send you more books from the series you have chosen, and bill you at our low, subscribers-only discount price. Harlequin® Romantic Suspense books consist of 4 books each month and cost just $5.49 each in the U.S. or $6.24 each in Canada, a savings of at least 12% off the cover price. Harlequin Intrigue® Larger-Print books consist of 6 books each month and cost just $6.49 each in the U.S. or $6.99 each in Canada, a savings of at least 13% off the cover price. It's quite a bargain! Shipping and handling is just 50¢ per book in the U.S. and $1.25 per book in Canada*. You may return any shipment at our expense and cancel at any time by calling the number below — or you may continue to receive monthly shipments at our low, subscribers-only discount price plus shipping and handling.

Chapter 10

At lunchtime, Luca was happy that Nicky and she joined Kathy and Chessie, who'd been working with, and looking after, her son that morning. Others who often were around them at meals sat on seats nearby, including Denise, Leonard and Bibi. Everyone had plates of food in front of them as well as glasses of water or other drinks, including coffee. Clearly, no one was going hungry. No one acted at all concerned about why they were there, under protection. Neither did Luca, of course, but she recalled it often, as she always did.

As well as the most recent threats she'd received from Morley. But she definitely wouldn't focus on that. She would rely on this shelter, and those in charge like Scott, to help her.

And…well, Mark wasn't in charge. He hadn't even

shown up for lunch, at least not yet. But he knew of those threats. And she felt like she could rely on him, too, to help keep Nicky and her safe.

Enough thinking about that. She had a meal to eat. A son to take care of. And the fun of watching as the people around them all paid attention to Nicky.

They praised him about how he was doing helping to train the dogs. Once, Chessie mentioned how proud she was of how well they'd done that morning. Luca laughed along with them, thanked them again for Kathy and Chessie's work with her son, and really enjoyed the meal, not to mention Nicky's obvious pleasure and pride when he was the focus of the conversation and applauded for all he had learned so far.

"I want to do more," he told them all, raising his hand holding a fork and gesturing toward the sky. "Lots of doggies. I want to teach them lots of tricks."

That earned him a laugh and more praise.

Luca's sandwich that day was egg salad. She'd also picked up one for Nicky, who seemed to enjoy it along with the pieces of fruit on his plate, though he might not finish it all. Everything tasted good to her.

Never mind that she worried about when they could leave, to give Nicky a future. Their present was here, and that, for now, was a very good thing.

As they ate, she noticed Scott and Nella came into the cafeteria and went to the food table to select their meals. Luca had a bunch of questions for Scott, mainly involving whether he had ordered the educational games they'd looked at online earlier, if so which ones, and when they were likely to arrive. That afternoon, Luca intended to stay with Nicky outside and help him work with the doggies until his naptime. But she looked forward to when the education she could work with him on included things that would help him learn even more of what children needed to know.

She was happy when Scott sat across from her, at Chessie's other side. Nella found a spot nearby.

"So," he said, looking at Nicky. "We're going to have some very special games here soon for you to play with. They'll help teach you lots of fun things, like more about the alphabet and reading and counting and adding."

He must have ordered the equipment. Luca wanted to cheer. "That does sound like fun, doesn't it, Nicky?" she said to her son. "It'll be like your preschool. You need to thank Mr. Scott for ordering those special games for you." She looked toward Scott, who nodded, clearly acknowledging he'd placed the orders. She couldn't exactly ask when the stuff might arrive, if he even knew. She had no idea where he was having them shipped, or if someone had to receive them and somehow bring them here.

"Thank you, Mr. Scott," Nicky said.

The man who was thanked grinned broadly. "You're very welcome, Nicky," he said.

Luca had the impression that the director of this facility would now be even more inclined to help rescue people with kids.

That made her feel good. Not that she wanted to be here, but if her living at this facility with her child made it even more accessible to other people with kids who needed protection, it made her proud to be a factor in getting them accepted.

But when would she and Nicky be able to leave?

When would Morley be caught as the sleazy murderer, and threatener, that he was?

She forced her mind back to the happiness she'd felt an instant earlier. For the rest of the meal she encouraged Nicky to interact with Scott and the others around them, telling them what he wanted to learn about doggies and letters and numbers. He knew some things about all of them, and was doing well for his age, but he still had a lot to learn as he grew older.

Luca was heartened that he'd continue his education here, hopefully well enough to succeed even more when he finally could go back to preschool, maybe, or at least kindergarten and above.

The meal went as quickly as most apparently did around here, even though Luca and Nicky had only experienced a few so far.

How many would they have here?

Time, and what happened outside this shelter, would tell.

They soon left the cafeteria, Chessie staying near them. "I want you to help me work with Spike this afternoon," she said to Nicky. "He's that German Shepherd, the former K-9 police dog, who knows a lot of commands and always obeys them, like the very special pup he is. And though I like helping train some of our less-skilled dogs needing new forever homes, it's fun to practice those commands with Spike. Okay with you?"

Unsurprisingly Nicky said, "Okay!" As they went

into the yard, he reached for Chessie's hand. Luca smiled at that. Her son was always trusting, and with the staff members around here, especially those who seemed to adore him and want to help him learn about doggies, that was fine.

Working with Spike should be fine. Yes, as a shepherd, he was a large dog, but from what Luca had seen of him, Chessie was right. He was well-trained. He seemed to like people and be gentle with them.

Although she figured if he was on the job as a K-9 and told to go after some kind of suspect, he'd do it well.

They went to get Spike in the building where he was located and were soon in the middle of the central area, near the building with medium-sized dogs, on the concrete pathway. Chessie stepped off it, onto the grass, Spike on one side and Nicky, still holding her hand, on the other.

Luca remained on the paving nearby, ready to watch. She wasn't surprised when several other staff members joined them, including Kathy with Mocha, the little terrier mix, and Leonard with Jade, the Great Dane mix.

Luca really liked dogs. She was glad to see her son did too. She had an urge now and then, like now, to go work with one of the dogs at this shelter but being there for Nicky was more important. She needed to get him inside for a nap soon. And cheering him on could help him do his best with the doggies for now.

She saw from the corner of her eye that a few other staff members were walking dogs along the pathway, though not stopping to train them. Maybe she, and Nicky, could do that sometime too. As before, she marveled at the variety of types and sizes of pups here, including Jack, the part Jack Russell terrier, and Oodles, the poodle mix.

As she turned to watch several of the dogs being exercised, she noticed Mark and Rocky exit the apartment building. So he had been in there. Presumably, he'd grabbed whatever lunch he'd wanted from his own unit, since the shelter helped the staff members keep their kitchens stocked with sufficient amounts to eat there if they didn't choose to visit the cafeteria.

What had he been reading that was so interesting he'd preferred to be alone than with other staffers... like her? And Nicky?

Well, that was his business, not hers. Sure, she could be curious, but he deserved privacy just like everyone else around here.

Although, if the opportunity arose, she'd ask him. Depending on what it was, after all, maybe she'd want to read the book or magazine that had kept him so occupied.

She considered taking a few steps toward him, to meet up with him and his dog on their route, but stopped herself. What if they were headed somewhere else? What if he didn't want to talk with her?

That, too, was his own business. No matter how the thought made her feel incredibly sad in those few moments.

Until he joined her on the pathway. "Hi," he said as Rocky sniffed her hand at her side. She petted the pup's head.

She said, "Hi to you too," to the owner of the Doberman—another dog of a different size and type around here. She pondered whether to ask how Mark was doing, what he had been reading, something to start a conversation. Instead, she just turned back to watch Nicky gesture to Spike, who immediately sat, ears alert, as if waiting for the next command.

"Looks like Nicky is doing a great job with Spike," Mark said.

"Yes, I think he is. I'm proud of him, as always."

"Makes sense to me."

Before Luca could reply, Chessie called, "Hey, Mark, bring your smart dog over here too. Let's see how my excellent trainee, Nicky, does with him."

"Guess I'd better do it," Mark said, aiming a brief smile at Luca.

"Guess so." Once more she had an urge to do something to also work with the dogs. Or at least maybe Rocky, so she could continue talking with Mark.

Though not now.

At least, not at first. But she noticed that her son was starting to look tired.

She approached them all and looked down at Nicky. "One more command," she said, "and then it's naptime."

He must be really tired since he didn't argue with her. "Okay, Mommy."

"I understand," Chessie said, and had Nicky tell Rocky to sit, which the dog did. Then she, Kathy and Leonard, all still there working with dogs, told her boy to have a great nap. And also let him know they looked forward to working with him again with the doggies, although maybe not until tomorrow.

Luca was surprised, and glad, when Mark said, "I'm heading back that way too. I just wanted to get outside for a short while before going back to my apartment."

"And reading some more?" Luca asked, wanting to ask a lot more questions than that. But Nicky was with her now. He petted Rocky once then took Luca's hand. They started walking back in the direction from which Mark had just come, Rocky and him joining them.

"Yeah. It's a great use of my time."

Again, Luca wondered what he was reading, but didn't ask as Mark held the end of his dog's leash, and they soon reached the apartment building.

They got into the elevator. Mark stood nearer to the buttons than Luca and pushed the one to the fourth floor.

They soon reached it and got off.

Nicky was really dragging, and Luca was glad he'd soon be heading to bed.

Mark obviously noticed too. "Hey, guy," he said, kneeling beside Nicky, "I think it's time for a piggyback ride, don't you?"

Nicky gave a sleepy smile and nodded.

"Okay, then, are you ready to pick me up?"

Luca's son's eyes grew wide. "Me pick you up?"

"Sure." But then Mark knelt with his back to Nicky. "Or I can pick you up instead. Just put your arms around my neck."

"Okay." And he did.

That made Luca smile. Although her son was thin, he was around thirty-five pounds. She carried him some, though it was more of a challenge these days as he got bigger. She loved the idea that Mark was not only picking him up but making a game of it.

As he knelt, Mark held out the end of Rocky's leash and Luca took hold of it. The Doberman clearly noticed as he looked up at her and wagged his tail. It was a long, thin tail. Luca believed that Dobies at least sometimes had their tails docked, but Rocky apparently hadn't, which seemed a good thing to her.

Although she wished she could watch from behind as Mark carried her son on his back, she knew she needed to go open the apartment. She and Rocky slipped in front of them and she soon had the door open. That gave her the opportunity to look back as Mark and Nicky approached. Nicky's face was visible over Mark's shoulder, and so was his thrilled but sleepy smile.

Luca gestured them inside and Mark maneuvered briefly so Nicky wouldn't hit his arms or head on the doorframe. She let Rocky's leash go after she closed the door, then led Mark down the hall to Nicky's room.

There, Mark turned and knelt slightly, allowing the boy to sit on the bed before Mark let go.

"Was that fun?" she asked Nicky.

"Yes!" he exclaimed.

"Then what do you—"

Nicky didn't let her finish. "Thank you, Mr. Mark."

Mark laughed. "Again, you're very welcome, Nicky."

"Let's go into the bathroom for a minute," Luca said, figuring her son would need to go. Plus, she wanted to wash his face and hands. He could sleep in his shelter T-shirt, blue jeans and socks for his nap. No need for pajamas that afternoon.

She didn't ask Mark for any unneeded assistance. She figured that by the time she got her son into bed, he and his dog would already have left.

But as she closed Nicky's bedroom door behind her a short while later, she was glad to see Mark and Rocky still in the living room.

"Thanks for helping Nicky get to bed. It's what he really needs at the moment."

"I figured," Mark said. He was standing near the window, Rocky at his side, looking out at the view over the center courtyard.

"Lots of staffers still out there walking dogs, I assume," Luca said. That had been the case when they'd been down there just a few minutes ago.

"Yep." Mark moved slightly away from the window, as if he intended to join them.

"Would you like a cup of coffee?" Luca asked hastily. She could understand why Mark might want to get back out with his own dog, although he'd indicated he wanted to return to his apartment. But she was hoping he'd stay at least for a little while.

So she could ask him some questions about his reading material. That was why she wanted him to stay, or so she told herself.

Although, she recognized the adult company—*his* adult company—would be appreciated. Maybe even enjoyable during this time while Nicky slept and she'd be on her own.

"Sounds good," Mark said. "A little caffeine never hurts."

"I agree." Luca headed into the kitchen, where she

started a pot brewing. She hadn't made any herself here since she usually drank some in the cafeteria, but she was aware of where her coffeepot was, as well as the coffee and filters supplied to her.

She wasn't surprised when Mark, with Rocky, joined her in the kitchen. "I've got some cookies," she said. "I need to make sure I've got plenty with my little guy around. Oh, and carrots too."

"Cookies will be fine," Mark said, sitting at the kitchen table with Rocky lying on the tiled floor beside him.

That pleased Luca. A lot. At least for the moment, he'd be staying, until he got his cup of coffee. Maybe a couple of cups, by the time she topped it off as they talked…?

Assuming they talked.

She sat opposite Mark at the small wood-veneer table, the package of chocolate-chip cookies supplied by the shelter in the middle, waiting until the coffee was ready. She could hear the water dripping in the percolator behind her.

She pondered how to start the conversation she wanted: *What were you reading?* Or *Would you like to spend more time with Nicky and me here?* Okay, the first question was fine, but she wasn't sure she wanted to hear the answer to the second.

"What do you think of this shelter now?" Mark, interestingly, was the one to start the conversation.

"I still love it," she said with no hesitation. "I really appreciate the fact Nicky and I are under protection here, and that we're being given so much for our safety and otherwise, like food. And coffee. And cookies."

She smiled and was pleased to see that his very handsome face smiled right back. Those blue eyes, beneath his thick brows, were amazing. And she really appreciated the ruggedness of his features beneath his short brown hair.

But where was his cowboy hat? Somewhere in this building, she figured, wherever his apartment was.

"Yeah, this really is a special place," he said.

"Have you been here long?" She still wondered what had happened in his life to bring him here.

How could anyone dare endanger this strong, handsome cowboy?

"Not really. I just had some bad stuff happen in my life, which I don't like to discuss, but I got involved with some bad guys who wound up threatening me. Enough said. I happened to hear about the Chance Animal Shelter, so here I am, at least for a while until those guys forget about me."

That was more info than Luca had heard before, but it lacked any detail for her to know what had really brought him here.

And how would he know if, and when, those bad guys, whoever they were and whatever they wanted with him, forgot about him?

She assumed that Scott, being the director and seeming to know a lot about everyone here and what was going on outside, would be the one to keep Mark informed.

"Got it," she said, though she didn't. "And you get to keep your Rocky here too. Was he much help with those bad guys?"

"Oh, yeah. But I worried that they'd hurt him."

That, Luca could understand. Although a dog like Rocky might be able to hurt them instead. Maybe.

"I haven't seen you work much with the other dogs here," she said, "but I'll bet you'd be great at it. Rocky seems so well trained."

"Yeah, he's a good boy."

They talked about Rocky and all the commands he knew.

Luca soon heard the coffee maker sputter. She glanced toward the counter. "Looks like the coffee's ready."

She stood and retrieved some cups from the covered shelves above the counter, then poured them some coffee.

"Milk?" she asked.

"No, thanks. Black is fine with me."

Luca wasn't surprised. She set Mark's cup in front of him then added a dab of milk to her own.

She sat back down. Okay. It was time to get her curiosity satisfied. "So tell me," she said, taking a sip of her hot coffee but watching Mark's face, "what's so interesting that you're reading that took all your attention for so many hours today? Maybe I'd like to read it too."

"Maybe, but I doubt it," he said right away. "I was a computer programmer in my former life, and the book I was reading was about the technology of computers, a bit about their history but more about where it's anticipated they'll go from now on. Technical stuff, but interesting."

"Oh. Well, I like to use computers, especially to get on the internet." As she wished she could do more of now. "And my background is in accounting, so I, of course, used computers in my career. I like knowing how I can use them in what I'm doing, but I don't necessarily need to know more about them or what they may do in the future—although I assume I'll have to find out to the extent I need to use them then." But that was enough technology for her.

Interesting that Mark wanted to know all the rest of that stuff. Maybe she'd ask about where he thought computers would go in the future, another potential topic of conversation for them.

They did talk more about reading for a while, especially after Mark asked her what she liked to read.

"Mostly novels. I enjoy mysteries and…well, romantic suspense." She wasn't sure what he might think of that, but she'd mentioned them proudly. Heck, even though she'd been in a bad marriage, the idea of real romantic relationships appealed to her.

Although she'd had enough suspense in her own life.

They talked a little longer, and Luca refreshed their coffee a couple of times, smiling as Rocky looked up at her each time she stood.

Then Mark said, "Well, I need to get back to my reading. Yes, it may sound dry, but it's important to me, and I like to take advantage of my free time here in some way, till I can get back to my real life."

"I can understand that," she said.

She stood as he did and walked him through the living room to her apartment door, Rocky at his side.

"So, will you be reading through dinner tonight?" she couldn't help asking.

"Nope, I intend to be in the cafeteria. I hope to eat with Nicky and you."

That made Luca smile.

And then she felt her eyes widen as Mark bent his head down.

His kiss was wonderful. Brief, but warm and suggestive and enticing enough that Luca had to make herself resist grabbing his hand and attempting to lead him to her bedroom.

"See you later," she said breathlessly as he pulled away, trying to ignore the heated reaction throughout her body.

"Yeah," he said, his hoarse voice suggesting, too, that he was thinking sex thoughts as well. "See you later."

Chapter 11

Mark hurried down the hall to the stairway, Rocky prancing behind him.

See her later? Oh, yeah. Mark would look forward to seeing that luscious lady later in a different setting. A nice, open area filled with other people, like the cafeteria. An unsexy setting where he wouldn't have an urge to take her hand and lead her down the hall to her bedroom. Never mind that her son was sleeping in the next room. He'd gotten that craving…and fortunately shrugged it off.

Not that she'd have welcomed it anyway.

Would she? The way she had kissed him back…

No matter. Sure, he was attracted to her, but he was on duty here, undercover. And as an undelegated part of his job, he had taken on the role as one of her protectors.

Rocky and he went down one flight of stairs and

walked into the hallway where his apartment was located, still seeing no one else. Not surprising, considering the time—late afternoon, when most staff members would be doing things to work with some of the animals here, just keeping them company if nothing else.

He ushered Rocky inside the apartment before shutting the door behind him. They wouldn't stay here long. Mark figured he'd spend some time outside before dinner with the staffers walking dogs, talking to them, listening to them, being their friend, which was an important part of his job. Also an enjoyable part. He'd ask seemingly innocent questions that would encourage them to slip up, letting him know if they maintained any outside contacts. They were used to him doing that, by hinting how he missed such things himself.

That he, of course, did not.

And talking to them would keep his mind occupied.

Out of Luca's apartment. And her pants—

Yeah. As if. "Here, let's get you a treat, Rocky," he said to his dog, who unsurprisingly alerted on the word treat. Going into the small kitchen, he also got himself a drink of water, recalling how good the coffee Luca made had tasted.

Heck, it was just coffee. The fact that she'd been the one to get it brewing had nothing to do with its flavor.

Time to go outside. He glanced at the table beside his sofa where his Stetson lay and considered putting it on. His boots too. But as much as he enjoyed his special outfit, it would be inappropriate now, as it usually was here. But he'd managed occasionally to put them on for a while and hide from most staffers, or amuse them for a while.

Right now, he had people walking dogs to talk to as he exercised his own dog.

They soon headed down the stairs to the ground floor of the apartment building, where he opened the door and led Rocky outside.

Right now must be walk time rather than training. He saw Chessie with Spike, Kathy with Mocha, Leonard with Jade, and Augie with Oodles, all of them not far away and heading in his direction.

Rather than waiting, he tugged gently on Rocky's leash, and the two of them soon met up with the group. They turned on the path to join the others in the direction they were heading.

"Hey, looks like a good time for Rocky and me to take a walk around here," he said as they joined Mocha and Kathy.

"You won't be alone, that's for sure," she said.

"How did your training go before?" That was how Mark led into a brief discussion with the thin, agile senior. He doubted she was experiencing, or causing, any issues at the shelter. He understood she'd been there for a while, and he talked to her before. But she was a good one to start with.

It wasn't long before he went on to talk with Chessie, while Rocky and Spike traded nose sniffs. Jade, the Great Dane, joined them, and Mark talked to young Leonard too.

He slowed a bit so he could also talk to Augie, who walked with Oodles. Although Mark didn't know much about the backgrounds of the staff members, he understood that Augie, with his wispy hair and hunched shoulders, hadn't been there long. He'd gotten the sense that the senior, who walked slowly but deliberately, had had a bad time with some family members, or at least Scott hadn't denied it when Mark had wondered aloud while discussing who at the shelter might have outside contacts they remained in touch with.

But no matter what Augie's background was, Mark hadn't determined anything to make him suspect the guy more than any others. And whatever the reason, Augie was under protection now. Safe. And enjoying walking with Oodles.

"So, anything exciting going on in your life?" Mark asked to get the guy talking. He figured he knew the answer.

"What do you think?" Augie tilted his head sideways to look at Mark. "What could be exciting here?"

Mark nodded. "That's a good thing, right?"

"Yeah, that's a good thing." Augie nodded as he looked down at the pavement then slightly sideways toward the small white dog he walked. He kept up with Mark, then said, "How is Rocky doing? I'm still surprised they let you bring your own dog."

"Oh, it's just the two of us, and when I ran into trouble, I wasn't about to leave Rocky alone." That was all Mark intended to say about his situation outside. And it was partially true. The trouble he'd run into was needing to do his job, and Rocky was his undercover K-9 as well as his best friend. So, no, he wouldn't leave his dog alone.

As they continued, they passed by a couple other staffers and their dogs. Mark considered catching up with them to start a conversation, but doubted he'd learn anything out there today to help protect the shelter. Maybe the shelter didn't even need more protection. That was the impression he'd gotten from Kara, after all.

He moved along with Augie and Oodles, Rocky attempting to set the pace a little faster but obeying when Mark gently pulled his leash back and patted his head. Soon they were walking, with Rocky on his right and the other two on Mark's left.

Until they nearly reached the end of the walkway.

That was when Mark's phone vibrated in his pocket.

He had the sound turned off. Staff members weren't supposed to have phones, after all. And his was the special on-duty number he was using these days. No one from his former life knew what it was.

But his superiors at the Chance PD had it. He'd given it to Scott, too, in case the shelter's director needed to reach him quickly.

Speculating who it was did him no good. And now his mind was swirling as to why someone would be calling him on his covert phone.

Was someone outside attempting to covertly contact one of the staffers and Scott was calling him to check it out? That was why he was here, after all.

Or had Sherm or Kara decided that nothing was going on at the shelter, that there was no further need for Mark to stay undercover?

On one level, he hoped that was it. But he doubted

he'd been here long enough for that decision to be made. He also doubted the quiet as far as supposed rumors or contacts had lasted a sufficient amount of time to cancel his assignment. Plus, they wouldn't call him about that but would ask to see him.

He was overthinking this, as he tended to do a lot on this undercover assignment. What he wanted to do was to answer the phone, except he couldn't here. And it had stopped vibrating.

But whoever had called might have left a message. In any case, he'd be able to tell who it was, assuming it was one of his contacts whose number would be identified on his phone. And even if it wasn't someone in his system, he could always call back and pretend to be someone else. That wouldn't work well, but at least he'd find out who it was.

Enough conjecturing. He turned to Augie, who remained beside him. "I need to head for my apartment for a bathroom break," he said, "and to rest just a little before dinner, since it starts soon. Will I see you there?"

"I never miss a meal," Augie said with a grin that crinkled his aging face even more.

"Good. C'mon, Rocky." Mark led Rocky to the side of the walkway, speeding up a bit. They'd already turned and were heading in the direction of the building containing the cafeteria and apartments, so that worked fine. He waved as he passed some of the people and dogs he'd walked with before, as well as others also walking. No one should be surprised when he headed into the building entrance. They all had places inside there, after all. And, unlike them, he didn't have to return the dog he walked to its proper place in the shelter enclosures.

He looked around in the entry. Once again, rather than ride the elevator, he led Rocky into the stairway and they walked up to the third floor, into the empty hallway and down a few doors to their apartment.

Once inside, he locked the door. He walked past the living room into the kitchen, farther from the hallway, so hopefully no one would be able to hear him speaking— although if someone did and mentioned it to him, he could always say he was talking to Rocky.

Only then did he remove his phone from his pocket and look at it. It indicated he had missed a call. He checked to see who it was from.

Sherm.

Sitting on his couch, he immediately pressed the button to return the call. Sherm answered right away.

"I assume you were in the middle of people or things as you're supposed to be and couldn't answer." The police chief's words sounded droll, but his tone was cutting.

"That's right. I got myself into my apartment alone, with no one around but Rocky, as soon as I could after I felt my phone vibrate."

"I needed to give you a warning. I've already talked to Scott about it and he said he would let Luca know. Not that I anticipate anything will happen on the shelter grounds…but the managers, and you, need to watch out."

That didn't sound good. But Sherm was contradicting himself by saying he didn't anticipate anything happening on the shelter grounds while giving some kind of important warning, as he seemed to be doing. And Scott would apparently warn Luca about whatever it was.

"Will do. What's going on?"

"Well, it's the situation with Cathleen—Luca, I mean. I heard back from Rudy Rincoll, the Cranstone police chief. He told me he'd had a meeting with Officer Boyle after we talked this morning. He says that Morley denied sending those emails, claiming Cathleen had sent them to herself and was attempting to set him up, that she was the one who'd murdered her husband, and now she needed a scapegoat to pin the murder on— which Morley had implied before. But he also said—and here's the important part—that he couldn't stay around there after those accusations, so he was taking a leave of absence. And then he left."

Mark rose immediately. "A leave of absence? Is anyone paying attention to where he is? Where he's going?"

"That's why I called you. When I called Scott, I told him the same thing. Advised that he might want to let Cathleen—er, Luca, know what's going on so she can be even more vigilant. Scott, too, of course. And you."

"Absolutely," Mark said. "Is there any way to get someone to check out whether the guy's just hanging out at his home while he takes his so-called leave of absence?"

Mark thought he heard Sherm sigh. "No need to. Even though Rudy apparently wants to trust his officer, he did send another officer to Morley's home to get him to sign some papers—after Morley didn't respond to some online requests. And…well, surprise, surprise. No one answered Morley's door.

"And I understand that, as a result, Rudy started looking further into the possibility of Morley's involvement in the death of George Almera, and may have uncovered some additional evidence. But he's also checking further into Morley's allegations against Cathleen."

"Wonderful. Well, hopefully he'll learn the truth, find and arrest the guy. But while he's disappeared, we need to stay alert around here—and everywhere in Chance."

"Got it."

"Meanwhile, I'll talk to Scott too. See what else we can do around here to beef up security—assuming Morley knows, or might know, where Luca is. Yeah, I'll do everything I can to ensure she and her son stay safe."

Everything. Oh, yeah, he meant it.

But he didn't know how. Not yet.

Well, first things first. "Hey, Rocky," he said after saying 'bye to Sherm as he reached for his dog's leash. "We're going out again."

Not to dinner yet, but to see Scott.

The director was alone when Mark got to his office. "Not surprised to see you here," he said as Mark entered with Rocky and shut the door behind him. "I assume you heard from Shermovski."

"Yeah, I did. He told me he contacted you too." Mark paused, then asked, "Have you told Luca about the conversation, and what's going on?"

"Not yet." Scott leaned back in his desk chair, shaking his head. "Maybe I should have. But I let Nella and our managers, Telma and Camp, know. Since it's almost dinnertime, I don't want Luca to hide out in her apartment with Nicky—now or in the future. They need to stay active here at the shelter as long as there's no indication Morley knows where she is and is after her here—although we'll assume to some extent that's the case and look after the two of them. With your help too."

He didn't make it a question, which was fine with Mark. Both Scott and he were employees of the Chance PD, although they both were undercover. It was their responsibility to take care of the staff members here under their protection.

That included Luca and her son.

Maybe there were no specific threats to the other staffers, now that they'd been given new identities and were living here under safeguard. At least Mark hadn't heard of any.

But the idea was to assume that any one of them could be hunted by whoever had endangered them before, and perhaps eventually located.

That possibility seemed more real, more timely, right now, with Luca and her son.

"I'll do whatever I can," Mark agreed. "Including heading out to keep an eye on Luca and Nicky now. I assume you'll want to take her aside at dinnertime or after to let her know what's going on. Or do you think it's better that she not be informed?"

He certainly hoped Scott intended to warn her. It wasn't supposed to be Mark's responsibility to do such things, especially when, in his covert persona, he was apparently just another staffer with no info beyond what the regular staff members knew.

But if Scott didn't—

"That's my intent," Scott told him. "Once we're through with dinner, I'll let her know what I heard, and also that we're being even more careful in the shelter and getting police to provide more outside patrols… Whatever it takes."

Like Mark continuing to visit the police station to discuss the situation with Kara and Sherm and, on the way, being even more observant as he walked Rocky downtown.

Oh, yeah, he would do all he could to ensure that the jerk, Morley, didn't get near Luca and Nicky, assuming he knew where they were.

Mark couldn't assume otherwise, no matter what he hoped and how secret and secure the shelter was.

For now, he thanked Scott for keeping him informed, said he'd look forward to joining the director as he warned Luca, then left the office, heading for the court-yard area.

He assumed Nicky's nap would be over by now. Maybe he and his mommy were outside now, working with dogs.

If not, they'd surely be out soon, if not walking or training dogs, then going to dinner.

He was surprised to see them exit the apartment building at the same time Rocky and he left the office building. Oops. What if Luca asked what he'd been doing in there?

He could always say he'd been summoned by Scott for some reason. Some innocuous reason, like a general update on how Mark was feeling here under the auspices of the shelter.

Or that he'd gone to ask Scott some equally innoc-uous question such as something about when people would be coming here next to potentially adopt one of the dogs. He could always say he wanted to be part of that process somehow, which was true. He would leave Rocky in their apartment for a short while as he helped meet with potential adopters in the entry building with one of the dogs he'd gotten to know a bit while exercis-ing Rocky alongside him.

Or—okay, he was overthinking this, as he tended to do. He didn't necessarily have to tell Luca anything.

But he did have to stay as close to her as he could, both before Scott informed her what was going on, and after as well.

It was still a bit early for dinner, but not for dog walking. Mark started in the direction Luca headed with Nicky.

"Hi," he said as he caught up with them. "Are you visiting with some more doggies before dinnertime?" He was looking at the child, presuming his mama would answer.

"That's what we're doing," Luca confirmed. "We don't have a lot of time, but Nicky hasn't visited the medium-sized dogs in their shelter area for a while, so I thought we'd go there to say hi before going to the cafeteria."

"Rocky and I will join you," Mark said, glancing into Luca's eyes, which fortunately appeared more amused than annoyed. "Maybe Rocky can say some-thing friendly to the other pups there."

"Really?" Nicky asked, looking sideways toward Mark's dog and holding out his hand.

Rocky sniffed it, and Nicky stroked his head.

"Really," Mark said, glad he had an excuse to stay in their presence.

Not that he assumed Morley would suddenly show up at the shelter to attack Luca.

For now, he couldn't assume otherwise either. He thought he'd feel a bit better after Luca was informed about what was happening, so she would stay even more alert.

The fact she was likely to become even more frightened? Maybe that was a good thing.

But Mark would do all he could to ensure she and her son weren't harmed.

Chapter 12

Oddly, Mark seemed to hustle Nicky and her quickly into the middle dog building. Other shelter residents were still walking dogs around them, but the way Mark took Nicky's hand and hurried into the building, checking to make sure Luca was right behind them, made her feel a bit nervous.

That was silly. There was nothing to feel nervous about. The kind man probably just wanted to help Nicky have some fun with the doggies before they headed to dinner.

Right?

She was probably just imagining that Mark was doing anything besides wanting to spend a little more time with Nicky and watch him react to dogs. The guy seemed nice, after all. And he also seemed to like her son.

Did he like her too?

It didn't matter, no matter what she felt about him.

And what did she feel? Darned if she knew.

They were inside the building near the medium-sized dogs now, with Rocky as usual at Mark's side. As with the one housing the smaller dogs, this one also had a concrete floor lined with enclosures along the side. Those enclosures contained raised platforms that held dog beds.

Dogs too. She knew the place wasn't filled, but there were about six dogs there at the moment. Luca recognized some as those being walked around since they'd arrived, though she didn't know their names, and she could only guess at their breed backgrounds. Although she really liked dogs, she didn't know much about breeds. But she guessed one they saw was a larger poodle mix than Oodles, who was outside. Another seemed to be part spaniel, and another maybe a schnauzer.

Whatever they were, she felt sorry for them. They were sheltered with at least a couple of other dogs but they still were…enclosed. No human company just then.

But maybe they didn't mind.

"Hey, would you like to play with Lallie?" Mark pointed to the spaniel behind the penned bars along with the schnauzer. She was gray with some white markings.

"Yes," Nicky said and clapped his hands.

In a minute, Mark had him outside the enclosure, but still on the inner walkway in the building. Did he intend to lead Nicky outside to walk or work with the dog?

Apparently not. Even though Luca had mostly seen interaction with the shelter dogs done on the grounds, they evidently were staying inside this time.

"Now, let me show you some tricks I do with Rocky, and you can try them with Lallie," Mark told Nicky. He glanced at Luca, as if asking her to help her son, which she had intended anyway.

Soon, they were doing some of the training exercises Luca had seen the shelter residents and dogs work on outside. Mark held his hand up to get Rocky to sit, and Nicky imitated him. Fortunately, Lallie knew enough to sit, too, and Nicky shouted in glee. Luca didn't even have to help him.

Then there was down and up and sit again. The dogs did a good job, and Luca was proud that Nicky did too.

And Mark? He demonstrated and smiled—and kept looking around the place as if he expected others to come in. It was almost dinnertime, so it wouldn't be surprising if some of the staffers returned dogs to this building as well as the others. Luca hadn't paid attention to the sizes of the dogs out there being worked with.

But there was something about the way Mark observed the door, as well as the windows, into the place. He didn't seem as if he looked forward to seeing whoever might enter, dogs or people.

He looked worried somehow.

What was he thinking?

He also kept looking at his watch. And in less than ten minutes he said, "Okay, we can head for the cafeteria now. Let's get Lallie back into her enclosure, okay?" He was looking at Nicky as if eager for his opinion, but didn't ask Luca if she was ready to go to dinner.

Well, she was. Not that she was starving, but she

could eat, and she would be delighted to help her son get his food.

Soon, Lallie was back inside with the schnauzer, whose name, according to the sign on the enclosure, was Beau. He seemed excited to have his friend back, and Luca couldn't help smiling as the two dogs traded sniffs and began walking around each other.

Mark said, "Let's get going, okay?"

Why was he in such a hurry now?

Did it matter? Luca was fine with getting to the cafeteria whenever.

Soon they were outside, where some staffers still exercised their dogs and others appeared to be taking pups back inside their buildings. Luca had the impression that most were getting themselves prepared for dinner. She wasn't sure who would take care of feeding the dogs that night or any other time, but she had no doubt that the canine residents of the shelter would also get their dinners. The other animals too.

"So, did you do anything new after we were together earlier this afternoon?" Mark asked as they walked the short distance. He held Rocky's leash, and Luca held Nicky's hand.

Strange question, Luca thought. What could she have done after that, besides going back outside to take Nicky to watch people work with dogs? And that was exactly what she'd done.

"What do you think?" she asked Mark, making sure her smile was at least somewhat pleasant. "It's not like I had a lot of time to do anything beyond what's now usual here—keeping an eye on Nicky while he napped, then coming outside. Why do you ask? Did you do anything different?"

Maybe that was why he'd asked. He wanted to reveal something exciting to her but wanted her to question him about it first, and so he'd asked her a question.

"Not really. But…well, you didn't happen to find a way to get online and check your email account again, did you?"

Her stomach clenched. Of course she hadn't. But had Scott made some kind of comment again about her disobeying him before?

Or—was there a reason she should have checked her email? She had a sinking sensation that she'd come up with the reason for the question.

"Don't I wish?" she asked lightly. "I'm still looking forward to the day Nicky and I can leave, and start our new life. For now, learning what's going on outside, including with friends who email me, might be a good way to prepare for it." Real friends, not like Morley, but she didn't mention him. Didn't even want to think about him.

They continued walking and almost reached the cafeteria.

"Maybe so," Mark said.

She had to ask. "Why did you ask me that?" Because he'd talked to Scott again about her prior mistake that hadn't really been a mistake? Or was there some other reason?

She believed he had a reason, after all, or why ask that?

"Oh, here we are," he said, hurrying ahead a few steps with Rocky without answering her question.

That made Luca worry all the more.

Well, this conversation wasn't done, though it was on hold for now. It was time for dinner.

The cafeteria wasn't crowded yet, so they would be able to choose where they sat. For now, Luca did the usual thing and accompanied Nicky to the table at the end. The main courses were baked chicken and mac and cheese. Luca put some of both on her plate and just the mac and cheese on Nicky's for now, since she'd have to cut pieces of chicken for him. There were also green beans and dinner rolls, and she got some of both, along with a salad for her and flatware for both of them.

She walked beside Nicky, who held his own nearly empty plate, to the area near the door where they usually sat. There, she got Nicky situated then went to get them both water.

She wasn't surprised when Mark took a seat next to Nicky, on his other side from her.

With him over there, she wouldn't be able to quiz him on why he asked that strange question before, since she'd have to talk over Nicky's head. But she probably wouldn't anyway, with the other staff members sitting near them at the table.

She'd simply have to continue wondering what was really on his mind. Hopefully, she would be able to ask him later.

Soon, Scott and Nella also took seats near them. Both greeted Nicky before saying hi to Luca or anyone else at the table, and Nicky seemed thrilled to say hi back.

Dinner progressed fine after that. Everyone seemed happy with what they were eating. They mostly conversed about how fortunate they were that the weather wasn't too chilly, even though it was an evening in May, not yet summer. It sometimes got cooler here, but it seemed to be in the fifties now.

There was some discussion about the next day, since Scott indicated they had a couple people from outside who wanted to come look at some dogs for possible adoption. But that could occur on Thursday or Friday rather than Wednesday. Whenever it happened, the staff members would need to stay in their apartments in case the visitors were taken into the shelter to look at the whole possible selection of dogs, rather than be brought just a few in the reception area. They'd have to later determine which would work best.

Luca had been told the protocol. As always, those in charge had to make absolutely sure that no one wanting to harm any of the staff members entered the premises in disguise as a potential adopter.

That would include Morley—but Luca still hoped he didn't really know where they were.

Luca noted that Scott shot a glance to Mark as he mentioned that, and Mark caught it and nodded.

What was that about? she wondered.

Yet another thing she'd probably not find out.

When they were done eating, Luca helped Nicky clear his dishes, and they hung around the back area of the eating room. Some staffers wanted to ask Nicky how he enjoyed his first days here, whether he liked looking at and working with the doggies, and more.

Luca had the impression those who spoke with him, like Chessie and Kathy and Augie, might miss their former lives where there might have been kids around, though she didn't have the sense any of them had their own children at home being watched by others. If they had kids, they were probably grown and out of the house. And hopefully not in danger.

She pondered if there was anything fun and different she could do with Nicky that evening, possibly with some of the other staffers.

But before she thought of anything, Scott joined her. "Hey, Luca," he said. "There are some things I'd like to go over with you, right now if it's possible."

Oh, yes, it was possible. And possibly troubling. Although maybe he just had some simple questions or ideas to run by her.

The idea of checking her email, as Mark mentioned earlier, rolled through her mind but she decided not to address that now.

"Sure," she said. "Do you want to do it here or—"

"Yes, here would be fine. And… Chessie, how would you like to take Nicky over to the small dog building for a few minutes so he can watch them get their dinner?"

Interesting, Luca thought. Scott didn't ask if that was all right with her. It was, but it also made her worry even more.

She wasn't surprised, and was in fact happy, when Chessie agreed and took Nicky's hand. She was joined by Bibi and Kathy, and all four headed out the cafeteria door.

And Mark? He simply waved and headed across the room, then outside with Rocky, disappointing Luca. But she did want to follow up with Scott.

"Why don't we go over here?" Scott asked, pointing toward the door into the kitchen.

Why? Luca thought. She would learn soon what was on his mind. And she had the sense it wouldn't make her at all happy.

She had been in the kitchen before but wondered why Scott led her there now. It was large, with brick walls and several refrigerators and freezers, along with a large glass stove, ovens, dishwashers and quite a few counters where food could be prepared. Doors indicated there was a pantry off to the side.

It was also enclosed. Was that why Scott had brought her here?

He stopped near one of the refrigerators and turned to look at her. "So," he said, "I need to keep you up to date on some things going on outside."

Outside. Away from this protective shelter. Luca felt her heart sink, even as she began trembling. With all this lead-up, she had to assume she knew what it was about.

"Is it something about Morley?" she asked. What else?

"That's right." Scott's blue eyes appeared concerned. And sympathetic.

That worried Luca even more.

But she wasn't going to display any of the fear she felt. Instead, she squared her shoulders. "So tell me," she said as insistently as she could muster.

He described a conversation he'd had with Sherm about George's former boss, the Cranstone police chief Rudy Rincoll, who hadn't given her the impression he was particularly concerned about Morley being a possible suspect in her husband's death.

But what Scott described now suggested he had changed his mind.

While Luca leaned on the refrigerator door, her hands clasped together as if that gave her the strength of someone protective holding them—not—he told her about how Rudy had had a conversation with Morley, apparently accusing him, or at least repeating that Morley had been accused by others, regarding the murder, and he remained under suspicion.

Morley had objected. And proclaimed his innocence, as usual. And again had said that Luca was guilty and trying to frame him. And the emails Luca had received? Morley indicated that she must have hacked his email account and sent them herself.

Of course, Luca thought.

Although the good thing was that Rudy hadn't indicated to Sherm that there was any evidence suggesting she had killed her husband. At least, nothing they'd found so far.

Unsurprising, considering her innocence. But Morley would be the one trying to frame someone.

Her.

At least he hadn't yet convinced anyone, apparently. A good thing. And the truth.

"Then he evidently told the Cranstone police chief that he couldn't continue to work there under those circumstances and said he'd be taking a leave of absence."

Really? "Well, it sounds as if there may be genuine suspicion about him there now." Luca attempted to act pleased. But she had to continue. "But what does it mean that he's taking a leave of absence?"

Was he leaving his job as a cop for now, hanging around there and attempting to get proof of his innocence? That would be false proof. But maybe he could get himself exonerated somehow.

That didn't sound at all good to Luca.

But the other thing churning in her mind was that a leave of absence would mean no one in the Cranstone PD would necessarily know where he was, unless they had someone monitoring him at home.

Where he wouldn't necessarily be. What if he was now somewhere out there—attempting to find her and Nicky?

What could she do?

"From what Rudy indicated, they tried to meet up with Morley at his home to get some paperwork signed. More likely, just to confirm that was where he was. But...he wasn't."

Luca took a deep breath. "He left his home?"

"Apparently, since I gather they tried to visit him a couple times without locating him. He might still be around there. The PD will most likely keep checking, or that's what I assume. But... Well, since Rudy was concerned about it enough to contact Chief Shermovski, who informed me, I figured I would let you know."

"Thanks," Luca said, sending him a sad smile. "I guess. But what happens now?"

His return smile was stronger, as if he wanted to make her feel better. "Nothing different. You're in a good, protective shelter, as you know. I'll be talking more with the officials at the local Chance police department, making sure they stay informed and vigilant.

We already get a lot of patrols circling around outside, some obviously cops patrolling the whole town and some undercover, but the point is that we're under surveillance to ensure that our residents stay safe."

"I know," Luca said. "This place is wonderful. I understand that everyone here, your managers and others in this special town, are doing all you can to keep all staff members here protected. I really appreciate it."

But she nevertheless wished they had more information about the man who had murdered her husband, and now appeared set on finding her and her son. To kill them?

Maybe, since Luca hadn't simply accepted the situation, and her husband's death, as something that happened on the job thanks to an investigation he'd been involved in.

She understood why Scott had brought her here by herself, with other shelter staff members watching her son. But she now had an urge to go find him and give him a hug.

Make sure he was okay.

"Anyway," Scott said, "maybe we didn't have to hide in here for me to let you know, but I didn't want to say anything in front of the other staff members at dinner. And going up to my office now might look a bit odd. But I thought you needed to know."

"Yes," Luca said sadly, "I did. And I gather there's not a whole lot more that can be done about it. Although... well, right or wrong, I think it would be appropriate for me to check my emails again, in case Morley is making some more threats there." As Mark seemed to suggest. A thought came to her. "Did Rudy say anything that might indicate Morley knows where Nicky and I are now?"

The very thought shot an additional bolt of fear through her, though she recognized that even if he did know, a lot was being done to protect all residents here, including her son and her.

Still…

"No, and we can't really know what the man's aware of now. All we can do is be careful. And… Well, I have to admit you're right about checking your email. I pondered it before but thought it better for you to stay away from it. You can't respond to anything, after all. And if you see more threats—"

"I can handle it," she asserted, hoping it was true.

"Well, all right then. As I said, I didn't think it was a good thing to go to my office tonight, but even if anyone notices, we can come up with a good excuse, maybe something about more information about the things we ordered to help Nicky learn."

"Sounds good to me." Luca made herself smile again even as her insides continued to quake at the idea of seeing any further threats.

Even seeing anything nonthreatening from that murderer…

Although knowing Morley, even something innocent in an email from him would seem menacing.

"Okay, let's go look on one of the computers upstairs. Someone might notice, but that's okay. You're all right with leaving Nicky with the staffers who're looking after him now, aren't you?"

Yes and no. She'd already thought about wanting to

have her son with her. Assuring herself he was happy and doing well.

But he'd be doing a lot better hanging out with the staffers and, hopefully, some dogs, than going upstairs with Scott and her.

Were Mark and Rocky with him now too? That would make her feel even better.

She might feel best of all if they were all with her. If she could have Mark's soothing, protective presence nearby as she continued to absorb this latest scary information about Morley.

"That's fine," she said.

They quickly headed out of the kitchen. Everyone seemed through with dinner, although a few people still hung around. A couple even said hi and went into the kitchen with arms full of containers of dirty dishes. Sara and Denise must have been waiting for Scott to finish so they could complete their cleanup.

Interesting that they hadn't come in. But maybe they were used to having Scott deal with people in trouble individually in places like the kitchen.

Soon, she and Scott were in the office building, and they went up the steps. He led her into one of the small empty manager's offices as he had before, where he sat on a chair in front of the desk and waved Luca onto the chair nearby. He started booting up the computer.

That was when Mark slipped into the room, Rocky with him. His face appeared angry as he looked down at them.

What was going on?

Scott asked him first. "What are you doing here? Something we should know?"

If so, how would Mark know it? Luca had wondered if there was more to the man than just being one of the staffers under protection, but hadn't focused on it. She believed her untoward attraction for him made her think there might be more to him than simply being in witness protection.

Or not so simply.

For now, Mark said, "You checked out Luca's emails yet?"

So he was still wondering about that. Was there something more on his mind than Luca had considered?

Apparently so.

"We're just about to," Scott said.

"Good. I want to know what's there too. I just got a really unexpected phone call, and there's something you need to know about." His focus was on Scott, not Luca.

He'd gotten a phone call? How? Staff members didn't have phones. Oh, yes, maybe he was more than a staff member.

Luca saw Scott look at her. "Guess you have some questions about…well, we'll deal with that later. For now—"

"For now, you need to know who I heard from and what I heard. Both of you, whether it's appropriate or not for Luca to hear. And I think, under the circumstances, it's more than appropriate."

Luca wanted to shake him. What was he talking about? He was looking at her as if his anger was directed at her, yet something in his eyes made her believe the opposite was true.

"What is it?" she asked, her voice raspy.

"I heard from your friend Mitzi," he replied, then looked at Scott, who appeared concerned. "She said you gave her my information, Scott, when she asked you for one of the staff members she could contact if she chose not to call you or a manager."

Really? Luca thought. Oh, yeah. He definitely was more than a staff member.

"She wanted to let me know, Morley attacked her and— Well, to save herself she had to tell him the truth about where Cathleen is."

Chapter 13

Luca felt her hand go to her mouth and her eyes tear up as she looked first at Mark and the dog beside him, then at Scott and back again.

Scott was looking at Mark, too, his expression grim. How horrible. In so many ways.

"Is…is Mitzi okay?" She absolutely hoped so. Mitzi was so kind, informing Luca about this wonderful shelter in the first place when Morley had stepped out of line. She was his fellow cop and could have just looked the other way.

Yes, George had also been Mitzi's coworker, but he was gone.

Murdered by Morley. And now Morley had attacked kind and caring Mitzi too.

"As far as I gathered when she called me," Mark said.

"And I understand why she caved, cop or not, but—" He stopped. He was standing over Luca as she remained in the chair facing Scott's desk. His expression appeared furious, as though he wanted to attack Mitzi for giving in and revealing Luca's location.

Luca understood that. Appreciated it.

But under the circumstances, what else could Mitzi have done? Died, maybe?

"That's good, then." Luca attempted to make her words sound strong, despite how her voice shook. "And…the fact that she mentioned this place when her own life was in danger. I'm so sorry she had to do that. I would do everything I could to protect this place and the staffers here. And I'm sure Mitzi would, too, if she could. But if that horrible Morley was threatening her life, I can certainly understand why she did it. Why she had to do it. Only now—"

"Only now, you're in even more danger," Mark snarled. "And now we have to figure out the best way to protect you—and this shelter—under these circumstances."

Luca felt a touch of gratitude and caring for Mark. He'd mentioned her before the shelter.

But if she could do anything to protect this place and the others here…

Maybe she could.

But first… "I need to go get my son," she said to Scott. "Or—"

"I'm sure he's fine. We'd have heard if there was any breach of the security, and the staffers watching him are good people. But… Here, wait a minute." Scott pulled his cell phone from his pocket, pushed a button and held it to his ear. In a moment he said, "Nella? Would you please go down to the yard and bring little Nicky up to my office? Chessie and a couple of others are looking after him."

Luca couldn't hear the answer, but Scott hung up right away.

"He'll be here soon," he told Luca, which made her feel better—at least a bit.

"Great," she said, knowing she sounded relieved.

Both men were looking at her with anxiety and compassion. And with expressions on both faces that indicated they were concerned for her.

It was Scott's job as director to protect her. And Mark? He was definitely protective, even as a staffer. Or whatever he was. He had to be more, if Scott had given Mitzi his information, right?

Didn't matter. What did matter was that she hoped to stay healthy and alive, caring for her son.

But if that horrible SOB Morley was willing to kill again just to get to her, he might harm others at this wonderful shelter.

She couldn't live with that either.

"I hate this situation," she stated. "But I'm just one of many, and I can't put others in danger too. In fact—" she looked at Scott "—I've no idea if Morley is still emailing me, maybe even saying now that he knows for certain where I am. Can I please check my email again?"

"Yeah, maybe that would be a good idea," Scott said. "As long as we're with you and can see what, if anything, the jerk said."

As long as *we're* with you? Interesting that Scott

included Mark in that. It only stressed what Luca had already been wondering.

Who was Mark really?

Well, that didn't matter now. She hoped to get more information, learn more about this man who seemed to want to ensure her safety despite his being here and apparently under protection. Along with his sweet dog— who might wind up being protective too.

For now— "So, which computer should I use to check my email?" she asked.

"Let's go to the one we used before." Scott stood, and so did Luca. He opened his office door and waved Mark and Rocky out first, as if they would scout the area to ensure there were no dangers in the hallway.

And there shouldn't be. Not in this wonderful shelter. Luca must be imagining Scott's intent in letting the other staffer lead, along with his dog.

Right? But...well, there clearly could be some kind of danger around here if Morley's apparent threat was to be believed.

And it was, considering the fact the man had attacked his smart and skilled coworker Mitzi to get information from her.

About Luca and her whereabouts—here.

Still, could the terrible man be inside this secure shelter? Surely not, and especially not this fast, considering the fact he'd only recently learned Luca's whereabouts.

But Luca was scared, and not only for herself.

Could these two men and anyone else charged with keeping an eye on this place protect it from a deranged killer like Morley?

That was assuming she was right, and kind, hand-some—and protective—Mark would help take on en-suring all was secure here.

They all hurried down the hall. No one leapt out to attack any of them, which didn't surprise Luca, although she was somewhat relieved as they entered the empty small office with the computer that she'd been allowed to use previously.

Scott sat in front of it first and booted it up, and be-fore he was done, Nella arrived with Nicky.

"Hi, Mommy," he said. "I was just helping with the doggies." He seemed to pout as if disappointed he'd been taken from his duties to come see her. That made Luca smile, even as she felt even more relieved that her son was now with her.

As Scott rose and motioned for her to sit on the chair he'd vacated in front of the computer, Luca was glad that Mark took Nicky's hand and led him to the corner of the small office along with Rocky, where they began giv-ing the dog the usual kinds of commands. Nella joined them. Nicky seemed thrilled.

So was Luca.

She looked away from them and toward the com-puter, where she logged into her old email address. She took a deep breath, hoping she wouldn't see anything from Morley—and if she did, she prayed it wouldn't be threats.

All her hopes were quickly dashed.

Yes, Morley had sent her an email. Just one.

And it was more terrifying than almost anything else

Luca had experienced since this all started—anything except the murder of her husband.

Morley's email:

Hello, Cathleen, it said. I know where you are. Well, I'm here in Chance now too. And I expect you to leave that damn animal shelter and join me quickly. You can bring your kid, but we're going to leave here. Together. Forever. If you don't? I've got a great supply of tear gas I can shoot over the fence into that place. Maybe I'll hit people with the canisters, or just get them to tear up. Will it kill the animals? Don't know. But it can do a bunch of damage and might hurt you and your kid and lots of others. So come out now. I'll be watching.

"No!" Luca screamed then glanced over at her son. He stared at her, his eyes open as if he was scared.

She didn't want him to be scared. She didn't want to be scared.

She looked to Scott, who stood behind her, reading the email over her shoulder. "What can we do?" she asked, her voice raspy.

Meanwhile, Mark had joined Scott behind her, leaving Nicky with Nella and Rocky. He, too, read the message.

"Damn," he said as Luca saw him lock eyes with Scott. "Time to find the SOB and make sure everything remains okay."

A lot easier said than done, Mark realized. And as much as he'd like to, he couldn't do it by himself. Not without more information at least.

It was a good thing that Scott was taking charge here.

While Luca joined her son, Nella led Rocky over to the computer desk with Scott and Mark. The director said, "First, I need to let our other managers know what's going on." He made some quick calls, disconnected and said, "They'll both be here in a couple minutes. Now we need to make the important call to the Chance PD that I'm sure you're waiting for."

"Exactly," Mark said. He pulled one of the chairs around the desk this time so he could sit behind it with the shelter director as he used his phone again to make another call. Rocky took his place on the floor beside Mark.

Nella sat on one of the chairs facing the desk, leaning forward in obvious concern. Mark agreed it was best that the managers here knew what was going on. And Nella, considering her relationship with Scott, would learn about it anyway.

Scott pushed the button to put the call on speaker as someone answered. It was Shermovski. Scott had unsurprisingly called the police chief.

"Hiya, Scott. What's new at that wonderful animal shelter of yours?" His tone seemed both amused and inquisitive. He of all people knew what the focus of the shelter was, and he would certainly know that Scott wouldn't be calling him to report on issues about the dogs or cats.

"Can you get Kara to join you?" Scott asked, glancing at Mark, who nodded. It would be much better to have both the police chief and assistant chief there to hear the current situation and help determine how best to protect the shelter—and capture the miserable suspect who was threatening it.

"Sure. Wait a sec." Sherm put them on hold, and Scott turned to Mark.

"I'll let you do the talking," he said. "You're the one who spoke with Mitzi. Although—" He glanced toward the corner where Luca played with Nicky, though she kept glancing at them as if she really wanted to know what they were saying too. Of course she would. Plus, they would probably talk loud enough that she could hear anyway. "I assume," Scott continued, "that Luca doesn't know your real background, but I think it might be time for her to learn."

Mark nodded. "Definitely."

"Hi, Scott. Mark." That was Assistant Chief Kara's voice. "What's going on? Nothing good, I assume, since you want us both on the phone."

As Scott looked at him, Mark began to speak. "Hi to both of you. This is Mark, as you probably know. We've got a bit of a situation. A bad one."

"Figured," Sherm said. "What's going on?"

Mark wished he could join Luca and plant his hands over her son's ears, but he assumed she'd keep him occupied enough not to be listening—he hoped. But he also hoped she would hear what was said from this end.

She needed to know what they were telling the local police, for her protection, and that of the shelter and its other inhabitants.

"Here's the thing. Remember that case we discussed that morning? Sherm, you gave me that update this afternoon. And now, well, we have an update for you."

"Really? So…what's going on?" Sherm asked.

"Well, that guy we were talking about evidently attacked another officer on that force who knows where Luca is, and now he's apparently here in Chance looking for her. He sent her an email telling her she better leave the shelter and go with him or he'd…he'd do something particularly nasty from outside the shelter that might harm it and all the residents, people and animals."

"Damn!" Sherm exclaimed as Kara said, "Oh, no!"

"Yeah. We wanted to let you know right away so you could beef up patrols in the area and search for the guy. He should be on the Cranstone Police Department website. As we've discussed, the guy's name is Officer Morley Boyle, although he's on a leave of absence right now. Hopefully, his picture is still there. If not, you should be able to get one from Chief Rincoll."

"We'll make sure to assign extra patrol cars in your area," Sherm agreed.

"And we'll have anyone brought in to talk to who seems overly interested in the shelter," Kara said.

That sounded good. But would it be enough?

Apparently, Scott didn't think so either. "I know you've carefully beefed up patrols around here before," he said. "And it's always helpful. But how about some undercover foot patrols as well? And maybe a few helicopter units deployed overhead that appear to be headed elsewhere but are watching and videoing the area? As long as nothing appears too obvious, since we still don't want to give away what this place really is."

"All of the above," Sherm fortunately agreed. "And yes, carefully. Though it's getting late now and it'll take a while to get all that going. We'll have a copter and a few cars out soon, at least. Foot patrols will likely need to wait until morning. Meanwhile, keep your security cameras rolling. And your doors and gates tightly locked, of course."

"Of course," Scott said. "And thanks."

"Thanks to you for all you do there," Kara responded. "Both of you."

That caused Mark to shoot another glance toward Luca. Was she paying attention?

Apparently so. Her expression appeared a bit confused, but she was staring at him as if she wanted to see inside his brain.

Well, he'd have to admit who he really was at last. Later.

He intended to spend the night with Nicky and Luca in their apartment, keeping watch. Even though what he really wanted was to take Rocky out and patrol around the shelter themselves that night, watching.

But even though the area, including the shelter walls, were well lit, the two of them were unlikely to find Morley if he was there. Oh, Rocky's wonderful nose would help, but daylight would be better.

Did the SOB intend to perform his attack that night? Hopefully not. He'd surely figure Luca/Cathleen wouldn't go out and look for him.

Although he could contact her again. Or try to. He wouldn't know she couldn't just access her emails at will.

Just then Telma and Camp entered Scott's office.

"What's going on?" Telma asked first. As they all

did, the young manager wore a Chance Animal Shelter T-shirt, hers a dark blue one, and jeans. "I was just on the phone talking to Kyle. He's got some possible dog adopters to bring up here in the next day or two."

Dr. Kyle Kornell was the veterinarian who took care of the shelter pets from the office near the entry. He visited as often as necessary for exams and to treat any ailing animals, but he also worked in a vet clinic downtown.

"Better let him know that we won't want any visitors here for a while, even potential good adopters," Scott said.

"Will do."

Meantime, Camp, also in a dark blue shirt and jeans, joined Luca and said hi, kneeling to bump fists with Nicky, who reached out to stroke Camp's long blond beard. Camp laughed and touched Nicky's chin. Then he straightened and turned, moving toward the desk.

Mark watched as Luca kept an eye on Camp, and on all of them, as she attempted to occupy her son's attention.

Both managers who'd just arrived sat on chairs beside Nella's, facing the desk. "So what's up?" Telma asked. She looked highly concerned, as if she recognized whatever it was couldn't be good considering how everyone had been asked to get together so quickly.

"I don't want you to stay here long," Scott said. "I need you to walk around the grounds, even after bedtime some. We've got a situation." He explained the communication from Morley to Luca, including the threats not only to her but to the shelter.

"Damn," Camp said. He looked across the room to where Luca, still watching them, continued to play with her son. The expression on his face suggested to Mark that he was considering telling their newest staff member that maybe she should obey the command of her enemy to protect this place and everyone else, but he quickly changed it to one of caring. "That's awful. Well, yeah, we'll do everything we can to make sure the jerk can't get in, and I assume you've already contacted the authorities to watch from the outside, right?"

"Right," Scott said.

Mark watched and listened as the people in charge of this shelter and its safety briefly discussed the situation further, then broke up to take care of their responsibilities and check to make sure all was in order inside the grounds.

Outside? Well, that was where the real problem was likely to be. There was not a whole lot any of them could do about it then, or maybe at all. But Mark would do his best tomorrow to look around and investigate with Rocky.

Tonight, though, he would hang out with Luca and her son in their apartment. He hoped she would be okay with it, but he'd do it in any case, Rocky at his side helping.

As Camp and Telma left, Mark tilted his head briefly toward the two people who'd be in his charge that night as he looked into Scott's eyes. The director nodded. He clearly understood what Mark was up to and agreed.

"Nella and I will join the others and walk around the

facility," Scott said. "The rest of you… Well, have as good a night as possible."

He was looking at Luca then. She attempted a brief smile but that didn't work. She said, "Thank you, Scott." Turning back to Nicky, she told him, "Now it's time to go to our place to get ready for bed."

She held out her hand and her son took it. "Okay, Mommy."

"Hey, Rocky and I are coming too," Mark said, also looking at Nicky but not directly at Luca. "Maybe we can play a game before bed, okay?"

"Yeah." Nicky sounded delighted.

Mark wasn't sure what kind of game. Maybe rolling a ball so Rocky could chase it along the floor of the apartment. He reckoned the kid would have a ball with his other toys.

He didn't carry one. But he did have his phone in his pocket.

And he'd make a quick stop at his apartment on his way to pick something else up and bring it along.

His gun.

Chapter 14

Luca—and yes, she wanted to still think of herself as Luca despite how the enemy after her referred to her by her former name—was terrified.

And not just for herself and her son.

They left Scott's office to go to her apartment. Mark was with Nicky and her, but at the elevator on the ground floor of the building, he said, "I'm going to my place for now, but I'll join you at your apartment in a few minutes."

She looked into his blue eyes. There was a sternness to them, as if he expected her to object to his coming over.

She wouldn't do that. She needed to feel as safe as possible, especially for Nicky. For now, at least. And Mark's presence would help with that.

But from the moment she'd read that email from

Morley, she'd had an urge, as terrible as it was, to run out of the shelter, leaving her son with those who could take care of him, and give herself up to the crazy, dangerous man who threatened everyone here. Yes, she'd be giving up her own life, but for a good reason. Many good reasons.

"That sounds fine," she responded to Mark, hearing the hoarseness in her voice. And it did sound fine.

He'd at least check the place out. It was unlikely that Morley could be there anyway. And even if Mark stayed the night to protect them, that wouldn't prevent Morley from doing as he'd threatened eventually. Maybe even sooner.

Still holding Nicky's hand, she pressed the button for the elevator. Mark and Rocky joined them, but instead of going all the way to the fourth floor with them, they got off at the third, Mark waving as the door closed.

Luca felt a shot of panic as she watched him leave. That was silly. She and Nicky weren't in any more danger than they'd been having with Mark and Rocky with them a moment ago.

Plus, he said they'd be joining Nicky and her again soon.

She believed him. She trusted him.

Though, as soon as the elevator door opened again, she held Nicky's hand and nearly ran down the hall. "Too fast, Mommy," her son said, but she only slowed a little until she could use her key card to open the door.

She gently pushed Nicky inside then closed the door behind them, knowing it automatically locked. She wished it had a bolt, but inside the shelter that would have seemed overly cautious. Before.

"Sorry, sweetie," she said to her son. She realized it was eight o'clock already. "It's almost bedtime. Let's take a bath first, then read a bedtime story."

"Okay, Mommy."

From the living room, she took Nicky into the bathroom then went to get his pajamas. As she returned, she heard a knock on the apartment door.

Her heart raced. Surely it was Mark, joining them.

But—

Okay, she had to check. "Stay in the bathroom, Nicky," she called to her son. "I'll be right back." She hoped.

Still holding his PJs against her chest, as if they would provide a touch of protection, she returned to the apartment's front door. "Who's there?" she called, hoping she knew the answer.

She did.

"It's Mark. Please let me in." The voice was that of the man who'd been in her life for the last few days, amusing her, protecting her, making her emotions rock in a good way compared with all the terrible things that were otherwise in her life.

"Okay." She immediately opened the door. Of course it was him standing there, tall and still in his shelter T-shirt and jeans, his rugged face looking down at her, his blue eyes crinkled in concern—and caring?

She hoped so.

He immediately slipped inside, not waiting for any verbal invitation from her, which was fine. After Rocky joined him, Mark was the one to turn and close the door this time, making Luca feel even more secure, which was silly. He couldn't lock it any more than she could.

But that sense of security was thanks to his presence.

"I've got to get Nicky into the tub," she told him. "Want to help with the bath?"

He blinked as if surprised at the invitation. "Sure," he said.

Luca was aware of Mark and his dog following her through the small and cozy living room and into the bathroom, where Nicky stood near the door. Her son's face lit up as he saw Mark enter, Rocky outside behind him. "You're here! Rocky's here."

"Yep. We wanted to help you get to bed tonight."

"Yay!"

Luca ran the shallow, warm water into the small white tub that had the showerhead above it, the sheer plastic curtain off to the side. She shut the water off before the tub got very full, then helped Nicky with his clothes.

Fortunately, her son wasn't shy about being seen that way. It only took a few minutes to help him get washed and shampooed, partly with Mark's help. Mark gently scrubbed Nicky's back with a washcloth after the boy looked at him quizzically, as if asking the man to participate.

Watching them, Luca smiled.

Soon, the bath was over. Luca toweled Nicky dry and helped him on with his pajamas with the cartoon rabbits. His light brown hair remained damp, and she retrieved a comb from where she'd put it in the medicine cabinet and untangled it.

"Will you read my bedtime story?" he asked Mark, who appeared delighted.

That also delighted Luca. She realized that was silly. Mark's participating here, tonight, was again only for their protection. He wasn't attempting to act like he was one of the family.

Was he?

Soon they were in Nicky's bedroom. Luca pulled back the yellow sheet with the brown blanket and floral bedspread on top of the single bed and then helped Nicky under the covers.

They didn't have many books with them, but Luca took a couple off the shelf in the small closet where she'd placed them when she'd unpacked the few things she'd been able to bring for Nicky. Both were classic Dr. Seuss books, which she knew he liked. He picked one, and she smiled and handed it to Mark.

"Looks like you're going to be the Grinch tonight," she said.

"I'm delighted." Mark accepted the book and sat near the headboard, where Nicky was propped up near his pillow. Rocky settled on the floor beside them.

Soon, Mark was reading in his deep voice that Luca usually found sexy. He was skilled enough to pretend to be the characters and seemed to be having fun, even as Nicky chortled and laughed and pointed to the pictures a lot.

Luca had fun too. She even forgot the reason they were there—well, not really. And especially not this night.

But she appreciated this aspect of protective Mark in

addition to all the other aspects she'd discovered about him in the short time she had known him.

Nicky was still giggling as Mark finished, but his voice sounded tired and he was sagging into his pillow. "More book," he managed to say, but Luca was firm as she removed the Grinch book from Mark's hand.

"Not tonight," she said. "It's time to go to sleep. We can read more tomorrow night." *We* meaning Mark? Who knew?

Tomorrow might be a very interesting day. Hopefully not too scary, but Luca wasn't assuming anything.

"Good night little guy," Mark said, bending to kiss Nicky's forehead before standing. Luca felt a small shiver of happiness. That seemed so sweet.

As if, yes, Mark was becoming a member of their family.

Which he wasn't.

Luca kissed her son good-night, too, and was glad to see Mark exit the room with Rocky. She followed and closed the door behind her. She liked leaving it open to easily hear if her son called her, but she didn't want him disturbed by any conversation she would have with Mark, and the apartment was small enough that their voices might carry.

Besides, maybe he would be safer if his presence wasn't obvious to someone who might come in— Enough. That wasn't going to happen.

Especially not with Mark and his dog here, assuming they remained overnight to provide that additional protection. Luca could hope, and assume, that would be the case.

Mark stood in the living room, waiting for her.

"Would you like a glass of water?" she asked. "Coffee isn't good this late, and I don't have any wine or beer to serve you."

"We'll have to bring some of one or both here one of these days, but right now water would be fine." He told Rocky to stay, and he followed her around the corner into the kitchen.

"I've got some cheese and crackers, if you'd like," she told him as she got glasses out of the cabinet near the sink. "Or some cookies or—"

"You don't have to feed or entertain me," he said.

When she turned back to look up at him, he appeared amused, and that expression made his face appear even more...well, sexy.

But she shouldn't even think of such things. Ever. It wasn't appropriate.

And especially now, when they both had to remain alert, just in case something happened at the shelter that was so important to them.

Where they both had to remain safe. Nicky too. And even Rocky.

"No," she agreed, turning her back to grab glasses from a cabinet. "I don't. But as long as you're here, I at least don't want you to become dehydrated." She took the glasses to the refrigerator and pulled out a large plastic bottle filled with water that was provided by the shelter. "Ice?" she asked.

He laughed. "No, thanks."

She handed him one of the glasses before motioning

him into the living room. She said, "There are a few plastic bowls here. Should I give Rocky some water?"

"That would be very nice, but some from the sink is fine."

Luca figured she could keep that bowl around, designating it as the dog's bowl.

That assumed Rocky would be here again, which meant so would Mark.

And that was a good thing.

Rocky was a good boy as usual and stayed by Mark's side, but he seemed happy as Luca filled the bowl from the sink across the small room from the refrigerator and placed it on the floor off to the side of the cabinet below the sink. The dog began lapping quickly.

That made Luca smile. And she noticed Mark smiling too.

She liked the way he smiled.

She liked too much about him…

"Hey," she said. "It's too soon for me to head to bed." Oops, not the best way to phrase that. "I'm not sleepy yet," she continued. "And I think we should talk."

She had a lot more questions she wanted to ask this man, after all. But would he answer?

At least he might hang out there a bit longer. And continue his protectiveness.

But more?

Oh, no. No more.

Mark was happy enough to accept some water to drink. He was even happier that this sweet woman was caring enough about his dog to provide Rocky a drink, even using one of the clean bowls that had been supplied to her at this place.

Damn, but he realized that too much about Luca made him happy. That only made him more concerned about her safety here, and her cute little son's too.

If only he had some way of tracking down the SOB who was threatening her.

He'd go outside the shelter tomorrow to keep a better eye on the place. He'd also stay in close touch with his superior officers at the Chance PD. And now he had his gun with him, too, stuck into his belt beneath his shirt. Yeah, he felt like a cowboy again.

Somehow, someone had to find Morley before the dangerous jerk could do anything to hurt anyone here at the shelter.

And especially Luca and Nicky.

He followed Luca into her living room and sat beside her on the gray sofa that had fluffy upholstery, similar to the one in his apartment, and actually felt fairly comfortable. He placed his glass down on the floor near him since the room's coffee table was on the other side, opposite where they now sat.

For now, all he could do was stay with her. He doubted there'd be an attack on her, or this place, tonight, but he wasn't going to take any chances.

In a while, he'd talk to whoever was in charge at the police station to check in and make sure they remained on alert, which he was certain they would after the updates Chief Shermovski and Assistant Chief Kara had heard.

"So tell me…" Luca said.

Her head was turned to look at him, he noticed. But, for the moment, he watched the wall across from them, beige stucco, no decorations, not especially attractive, yet he had to look somewhere, not at the lovely woman beside him.

"Tell you what?" he asked, forcing himself to look at her, and recognizing how difficult it was. He wanted to do a lot more than look at her.

He knew better than that.

"Who are you really, Mark the Supposed Staffer?"

That made him wince. Okay, he hadn't acted completely like those who were here under protection. And he'd sort of admitted to more when he'd talked about his conversation with Mitzi.

He recognized that Luca was an astute, intelligent woman he'd made it his job to help take care of more than the others here.

It was time to tell her who he really was.

Still…

"That's me," he replied, attempting to keep his tone humorous. "Mark. The. Staffer. I'm pretty much just like you, here under the protection of this very special shelter, and so's my sweet dog Rocky."

That dog had followed them in after taking his drink and now lay on the wooden floor near Mark's feet. He put his head up when he heard his name, and Mark petted it. Rocky sank back down.

Mark wished he could sink down a bit too. Luca was staring at him with an almost angry expression on her face; there was something about her lovely hazel eyes that seemed to bore inside his head.

"Then why does Scott treat you as if you're one of the managers? He lets you sit in on conversations with the local police. Regular staffers wouldn't be able to do that. And you were the one Mitzi called after she was given your contact information—and you have a phone, unlike the rest of us. And even the fact that you're able to keep your own dog here—" she looked down where Rocky lay and gave him a quick, soft pat on the head "—isn't the usual. So, like I said, who are you?"

"Okay," he said, leaning forward and staring her straight in the eye. "I figure I can trust you, but will you promise to keep what I say to yourself?"

She appeared a bit taken aback, as if she'd expected him to argue more. Or was she concerned about whether his trust of her would be justified?

He hoped not the latter. He felt a bit better after her response. "I promise I won't tell anyone what you say." But she continued to look worried. Maybe she thought he was going to admit something bad, like he was here because he'd killed someone but was nevertheless being protected.

Though he hadn't killed anyone—yet—there had been times in his career he'd been forced to shoot suspects to bring them down.

"All right, then." He leaned back on the sofa, wishing he had his Stetson on under these circumstances. After all, she'd already seen him in it, and he was about to reveal more of his background that had originated with him becoming a cowboy in his home state of Texas. "Here's the truth. I'm an undercover cop."

She leaned toward him, shaking her head, though

not in a negative way. "I kind of figured. But tell me more. Is Rocky a K-9? Why are you here at this shelter? And…" She hesitated.

"And what?" He knew his voice sounded droll. "Aren't you going to guess why I'm here?"

"Well…sure." Her eyes gleamed, and her lovely full lips puckered into an excited smile. "You got here long before I did, so it has nothing to do with what's going on with me. So, either one or more of the other staffers is in more danger than the Chance Animal Shelter can be sure of fighting off, or—" Her expression suddenly grew grim, almost frightened. "Are any of the staffers endangering the others? Are you trying to figure that out before anyone gets hurt?"

He wanted to give her a big, comforting hug, but he stayed where he was.

"Actually, the specifics are confidential. And, yes, I recognize that my status is confidential, too, and I shouldn't have admitted anything to you. But you're clearly observant, and I assume it would be okay to acknowledge what you have figured out about me, and Rocky too. But that's as far as I can go. The main thing, though, is that in addition to my official undercover assignment here, I've made it clear that I will do all I can to protect all staff members here, and now that definitely includes Nicky and you. Under the current circumstances, it's especially the two of you."

She leaned toward him now on the sofa, her expression suggesting gratitude. And more. Caring?

No, he couldn't assume anything like that.

"Then…then I was right," she said, her voice soft

and emotional. "Not that it was so doubtful, especially considering all that I saw tonight. But… Well, I know, right or wrong, that I've started to rely on you. And I appreciate your watching out for us. Especially— Well, I don't know what's likely to happen tomorrow, let alone tonight. But with you watching out for us, I feel… I feel that somehow…somehow, we'll be all right."

He wasn't sure who leaned closer first, but suddenly their arms were around each other. Her mouth was on his, sweet at first, and then their kiss grew warmer. They both stood, and he felt her body tight against his as his own began to react in a way he knew was wrong. But it absolutely felt just right.

Except…it wasn't enough.

He pressed himself closer against her curves and she seemed to push harder against him. Damn. She might feel his gun—but so what?

He tasted her tongue as he couldn't help speaking, hearing the hoarseness of his voice as he asked, "Can we go into your bedroom? And close the door? We can be quiet and listen for Nicky…and anything else."

He wondered, as he'd said it, if his alluding again to the trouble that brought him here would spoil it all, make her retreat. It should have made him back off, even though she'd referred to it first.

But he felt himself grow even harder as she said, "Oh, yes," and backed away, looking at him with those hazel eyes grown hot and misty as she took his hand and began leading him down the hall.

Chapter 15

This was a bad idea, Luca thought as she led Mark into her bedroom and closed the door behind them, listening for any sound from Nicky's room first. Silence, fortunately.

No noise from anyplace else that she could hear, either—no sound of tear gas canisters or people yelling… Yes, she hadn't stopped worrying about Morley's threats.

Still, bad idea or not, her body was yearning to feel Mark against her again. And more.

He left Rocky in the kitchen and told him to stay after giving him a dog treat from his pocket. When they'd kissed before, she'd noticed how much that pocket bulged. A lot of dog treats? Maybe that was where his hidden phone was too.

But that wasn't all. He hadn't mentioned it, but it seemed appropriate now that he had admitted who he really was.

He also had a gun tucked into his belt.

She hadn't noticed anything like that before tonight. Of course not—a shelter staffer, or someone who at least was supposed to look that way, walking around armed? Maybe that was why he'd gone to his apartment before coming here.

Another way for this cowboy cop to help protect her...

She felt another surge of caring—and heat—and turned to grab him. But he pulled her into his arms first. And began another kiss that she quite happily joined.

Heat surged through her, and she stepped forward enough to feel Mark's erection against her. It seemed to grow as they stood there and drew even closer.

Almost as if one or the other had issued an invitation, they both began edging toward her bed. It was the largest piece of furniture in the room; queen-sized, with a flowered coverlet and beige sheets, and a medium-height wooden headboard.

At the moment, it seemed to beckon her to bring the hot man still kissing her there so she could be with him and—

Before they reached it, Mark's strong but soft hands began lifting Luca's shelter T-shirt over her head. She raised her arms to help, and when it was off, she began doing the same with Mark's shirt.

He also helped her. She felt herself gasp in heat and delight when she saw his hard, muscular chest bared. Oh, yes. All masculine. All cowboy, maybe? She didn't know, but even seeing him partly unclad like that only added to her surge of need.

"Should we—" she began, then stopped as Mark bent and began pulling her jeans down. "Oh, yes." She gave her own response, even though that wasn't exactly the question she'd begun to ask.

She reached for his pants, but he backed away. He was the one to remove his own belt—and the gun he had stuck into it. He placed it carefully on her dresser along the wall.

Luca knew little about guns, even though her former husband, also a cop, had had his own. Mark's resembled the Glock that George had introduced her to and even suggested teaching her how to use. She hadn't wanted to, but recently she'd wished she'd taken instruction from him.

And she was appalled at where her mind was going now when she had so much else on her mind...

"You okay?" Mark asked. "Does my gun scare you?"

"No," she said. She didn't want to mention her deceased husband's weapon. She didn't want to even think about her poor, dead husband, especially not now. "But I'm glad you put it out of the way for now so we can—" She again stepped closer to tug at his pants. She soon got them down on the floor and then reached up to do the same with his boxers.

No need. He was already pulling them down to reveal his erection. It was stiff and large, and made her body rock with an invitation for more.

"Oh," she breathed and reached to pull away the scant remainder of her own clothing. But again, no need.

Mark was gentle yet firm as he took off her bra, then her panties.

She wasn't certain who moved first or how, but they were suddenly on top of the bed. She didn't even try to burrow under the covers. She could see so much better here—and she definitely wanted to continue to see Mark's sexy body, muscular from his arms down.

There was his large, enticing arousal that she was able to look at now as his hands started stroking her body, starting at her newly revealed breasts that reacted to the touch even as she, too, began touching him, from his hard chest muscles, then downward until that erection was in her hand.

She squeezed him gently, began pumping as he reached down to her eager body. She groaned as he caressed her there, softly at first, then more suggestively, touching inside her as he groaned, while she continued to touch him.

In moments, he moved away. Her groan grew into a sad sigh. Was he seeing reason, stopping what they were up to, as they should?

No, the guy was even more appealing as he retrieved his pants from the floor and pulled out a condom.

Smart, caring—and still utterly sexy—man.

He was back nearly immediately. He snuggled his hard body up close to hers and looked down at her with those blue eyes so seductively that she once more took hold of his erection.

That, as he moved on top of her, grew very close to the part of her that yearned for his entry. She pulled her hand away and allowed him to stroke her first as she moaned before he thrust himself inside her.

She was blown away at the way their sex continued, enjoying the feel of him, the sound of his sensual groans.

She felt herself reach climax even as his groaning stopped with a quiet gasp.

They lay still in each other's arms. Luca felt tired, relaxed—and sated. And thrilled that, even though she knew better and that this should never have happened, it *had* happened.

This once. Maybe never again. But at least she had this experience.

"Wow," she heard herself say softly.

"Yeah," Mark said and tightened his grip again.

Luca remained still for a while, her head on Mark's hard chest as it went up and down with his now-slowing breathing. She felt her breasts against his side, and she couldn't help feeling additional warmth again.

She wanted to stay that way all night. Well, after showering and changing into PJs and getting under the covers. Snuggling with this man as they slept.

And maybe they would. But now, she did have to get up. Put on her robe, at least, and go check on Nicky.

As they lay there, she'd been listening for him again, as always, as well as for any other sounds.

She'd heard nothing, which was a good thing. But she still had to peek in on him.

And so she said to Mark, "I'd better—"

He was on the same wavelength. "We'd both better get up. I'll get Rocky and go check to make sure nothing's going on at the shelter, and you can take care of Nicky."

"Exactly," she agreed, even though it was difficult to move away from this amazing man and stand up.

They hadn't shut off the bedroom light, so she couldn't help staring once more at Mark as he pulled on his boxers, pants and T-shirt. She also couldn't help feeling a bit sad as he covered his most sensual area. Well, at least she had this experience, even if she never again had the joy of observing his masculine charms that way.

His pants pocket remained a bit bulgy, apparently with his phone. He picked up the gun he'd placed on her dresser and stuck it back into his belt. That made her wince, although she tried not to show it. Better that he had a weapon to protect all of them.

She knew he was also watching her as she got up and tugged her robe from its hanger in the closet. She pulled it on slowly and teasingly, watching him, too, as he observed her hide her naked body beneath the soft, lacy fabric.

The look in his eyes made her want to lie back down with him right then and start another hot, enjoyable sexual encounter.

But that wasn't going to happen. Not now, at least.

Could she look forward to it later? She doubted it. Once was more than enough, or it should be.

Most important was to ensure that they, and every-one else here, were safe. She anticipated Mark leaving her apartment, at least for now, and probably for the rest of the night.

And so she just smiled at him, fastened her robe in the front, turned her back on Mark and headed for the bedroom door.

She stopped outside Nicky's room, listening. She still heard nothing, but she opened the door quietly and looked in.

Her son lay there on his bed, appearing sound asleep, as he should be.

Luca allowed herself a brief sigh of relief then closed the door again, leaving it open a slit this time so she could hear better if Nicky stirred.

She walked down the hall to the living room, where Mark had gone after retrieving Rocky from the kitchen.

"So," she said as brightly as she could. "Guess you'll be leaving now, right?"

"Right," he agreed, making her heart plummet even though it was the anticipated answer. Her spirits rose again right away as he said, "I'm going to get in touch with Scott, check out the shelter grounds with Rocky and make sure all's well. But after that, we'll be back, so if you go to sleep, make sure you're able to wake up and let us back in."

"Of course," she said, smiling broadly.

First, Mark returned to his apartment with Rocky. Good thing he'd fed his dog at the same time people had their dinner, since it was getting late.

He couldn't help thinking about the last hour. Too short and yet altogether worth it. Luca was one wonderful, beautiful, sexy woman, and their time making love had been more than awesome.

It was phenomenal. And, he believed, it could prove addictive if he allowed it to.

Enough of that. True, he wanted more, but what they'd done was inappropriate and they both knew it.

Sure, he'd return to her apartment later, but the goal remained to keep Luca and her son safe. And that was all.

For now, he quickly sat on the sofa that resembled Luca's and called Scott. "Hey," he said. "I've been keeping watch over Luca and Nicky in their apartment—" That was true, but not everything he'd done. "All seems okay, but Rocky and I are about to patrol the grounds inside the shelter. We could go outside but I'm concerned we'd be too obvious as targets at night. I assume the Chance PD has sent patrols as Sherm promised, right?"

"Yes, I've checked with him. Plus, I requested that he have the patrol officers call me as they pass by to report on what they see, and a half dozen have done just that. None have seen anything out of the ordinary— other cars going by, a few people walking dogs in the park, that's all."

"Any of them could be our suspect," Mark said through gritted teeth.

"Yeah, but with cops patrolling, it'd be harder for him to do anything. We just have to stay alert, and so will the CPD."

So Mark hoped, but he didn't like to rely on anyone. Not when so many people he cared about could be in jeopardy.

And most especially one of them. Well, two of them.

"Anyway, you caught me outside doing just what you

said you intended. Nella's with me. Why don't Rocky and you join us? We're in the medium dog building."

"Will do."

Before leaving, Mark checked himself out in his bathroom mirror to make sure nothing appeared to show...well, what Luca and he had just been up to.

He took Rocky into the kitchen and motioned to the water bowl on the floor, and the dog took a drink. Mark also gave him a dog biscuit as a treat and put a couple more into his pocket, on the other side from where he'd just returned his phone.

He also touched his weapon. Not that he really needed to assure himself it was there, but it did feel good to confirm that.

"Okay, boy," he said to Rocky.

The two of them exited via the apartment door, which he ensured was locked behind them. He saw one of the staff members entering an apartment at the end of the hall, but didn't want to talk, so he turned and led Rocky to the stairway, where they made their way down.

Because it was late, no one was out walking dogs. No one but him. He headed out of the apartment building and along the walkway at the shelter's center toward where the middle-sized dogs were kept. Not seeing Scott or Nella outside, he went inside the building and wasn't surprised to find them there.

They each had a dog on a leash beside them, Scott with the former K-9, Spike, and Nella with the spaniel, Lallie. Other dogs remained in the enclosures behind them, looking out.

"Are you going for a walk?" Mark asked them.

"It always helps to have a dog along while watching for anything out of the ordinary," Scott said. He looked down at Spike, then over toward Rocky. "Especially well-trained K-9s like these two. But it doesn't hurt to have another dog along as well." He reached down and gave Lallie a pat on her head.

Mark couldn't help looking at the other dogs who were watching them. He had an urge to reach in through the bars and pet them all. But that wasn't why he was there. Why they were there.

It was time to walk around the shelter to ensure everything was okay.

Apparently, Scott thought so too. He began leading them to the door of the building, Spike at his side. As usual, the director was wearing his denim work shirt with a red-and-brown Chance Animal Shelter logo on its chest pocket, complete with the outline of a dog, over his jeans. His long face appeared determined, as if he was certain they'd find anything that needed to be found inside the shelter grounds.

Mark hoped so too.

And Nella, clad in another Chance Animal Shelter T-shirt like Mark's, a green one, joined him right away. Mark had noticed that the pretty lady with the dark brown hair had similar dark eyes that seldom seemed to leave Scott when they were together. Like now.

Mark and Rocky brought up the rear after he closed the door behind them. Mark already observed the darkness outside on the shelter grounds, as usual illuminated by bright lights beaming down into the center of the walkway, even though none of the staffers were supposed to be out walking or training any of the dogs at this hour, nearing ten o'clock.

The air felt slightly cool and damp, and smelled somewhat sweet, as if something that had been baked in the kitchen behind them now permeated the outside a bit. Mark had experienced this before when it was overcast, as it was tonight. Even the dogs seemed somewhat interested, noses in the air.

But no reaction by any of them suggested any people were out and about when they shouldn't be.

Plus, like the dogs, Mark remained alert, listening for anything inappropriate. No voices. No sounds of anyone walking or moving or calling out to animals, or otherwise, except their own footsteps on the concrete.

The place seemed just fine. And he didn't hear anything that came from outside the perimeter fencing.

He wasn't the only one who seemed to be listening. Both Scott and Nella appeared to look around, sometimes in the directions the dogs they walked were looking, and often in other ways. They each seemed focused and determined, as was Mark.

Nothing.

That was fortunate. But it also was somewhat disturbing. They all knew the shelter could be a target of a deranged killer who was after one of those who lived there and apparently would stop at nothing to get her into his presence.

And if he did? Mark didn't even want to imagine what Morley might do to Luca—although his mind kept circling around all sorts of horrible possibilities.

No. That wouldn't happen. He was glad Scott and

Nella and the Chance PD, at a minimum, were doing a lot to prevent it.

So would Mark. He would do anything, everything, to keep Luca and Nicky safe.

They remained quiet as they walked, as Mark had anticipated. They also remained outside for nearly an hour, moving slowly but with determination.

All of them had protection in mind.

In theory, they could do this all night, but Mark realized they wouldn't. If he thought it would help them catch Morley, he'd have had no qualms about staying out here, walking and listening.

But soon Scott drew his phone from his pocket. The call he made was probably to someone at the Chance PD, considering what Mark heard him saying in a low voice—asking how patrols were going now, and whether they'd continue all night.

Apparently, he was satisfied, as he stopped walking and waited while Nella and Mark gathered around him.

"I think it's okay to go back inside," he said. "I confirmed that this place is under constant observation. And with our many security cameras and all, we'll be notified one way or another if there are any attempts to break in, or hurl things inside from beyond our perimeter."

"I definitely hope so," Mark said, "but—"

"I understand your *but*, and I'll want to have our other managers, and ourselves, remain on the lookout as constantly as possible. But for now, it won't help for us to get exhausted. We should head to bed and rely on the outside authorities."

"Really?" Mark let his skepticism show.

"You know that at least those in charge at the Chance PD know what this place is about, and they also know about this latest threat," Nella said. Her pretty face appeared strained, but she was nodding slowly. "They've probably notified at least some of their other officers, too—hopefully trustworthy ones. I think Scott's right. For now, we need to rely on them so we can get some rest tonight. We'll figure out what to do tomorrow to continue with our safety."

"You're right," Mark said, hoping they really were. Well, for now, he knew what he would do.

They walked back to the building housing the medium dogs, where Lallie was returned to an enclosure.

Scott kept K-9 Spike with him. "This pup will remain in the apartment building with us tonight. He's smart enough to bark if he hears anything out of line. Rocky, too, I expect."

"Definitely," Mark said.

Soon, they parted ways inside the apartment building. Mark knew Scott and Nella had a place downtown where they mostly lived, but they maintained a couple units here if they had to remain overnight for the safety of the staffers.

As they did that night.

"Good night," they both said as they headed down the first-floor hallway.

Mark didn't tell them where he would spend the night, but he figured they knew. He'd obviously started acting as special protector to Luca and her son.

And they didn't know about the activities Luca and he had engaged in earlier, though they might suspect.

He walked Rocky up the steps to the fourth floor right away, not bothering to stop at the third floor to visit his apartment.

Sure, he could bring his Stetson along and even wear his boots tomorrow, but why?

He enjoyed them, but didn't need them to behave like the protective, bold cowboy that he was, thanks to his background.

Now, he would use his heritage, his knowledge, his training and everything else within him to do his job here, remaining undercover to the extent he could—but making sure that this shelter, and most especially Luca and her son, stayed safe.

Or die trying.

No. He erased that from his mind. He intended to live for a nice, long time. With Luca in his life as much as possible, although he knew better than to assume they'd go to bed together again.

"Come on, Rocky," he said as they reached the fourth floor hallway. He led his dog down it and knocked on Luca's door, seeing no one else around and not hearing a thing from any of the units.

Not until he heard Luca call out, "Who's there?"

"Rocky wants to come in to see you," he replied. "I'm just keeping him company."

Luca laughed as she opened the door. She looked down. "Come on in, Rocky," she said. And then she looked up into Mark's eyes. Her expression was almost lustful, at least for a second, until she moved away and motioned for him to enter. "You come on in, too, Mark."

He did. And after ensuring the door was locked behind him, he took Luca into his arms. Their kiss was long and sexy and reminiscent of what they'd experienced before.

Mark wondered how this night would go.

Chapter 16

Mark was here to protect Nicky and her. Again. Still.

Not for any other reason, and it was best that way.

Even so, Luca couldn't help inviting him to her bedroom.

Sure, he could hang out in the living room, but it would be easier for him to ensure her safety if he was close to her, and Nicky's room, too, right next door. Plus, it would be okay if he also got some rest.

Or maybe that all was just an excuse. If he was here, she preferred having him remain in her company.

Nothing else. Not again.

Although if it happened…

Mark brought Rocky along with him to the bedroom, which was fine. Luca liked the Doberman.

She liked the dog's owner even better. But so what? She'd changed into her PJs before she'd headed to bed before. Nothing sexy about the long-sleeved, cotton, red-plaid shirt and matching pants. It was better that way.

"Everything okay outside?" she couldn't help asking.

"Yes, it looked that way. I met up with Scott and Nella. We walked around the shelter for a while. They had dogs along, too, and one of them was Spike."

The former official K-9. Probably a good companion for that kind of walk around the grounds under such disturbing circumstances, along with Rocky too.

She was curious though. "Who was the other dog?"

"Lallie."

"The spaniel, right?" As far as Luca knew, that dog was cute but wasn't necessarily protective.

"That's right. She was mostly keeping us company."

Luca found it interesting that, without asking her—and without even giving her a hug—Mark sat on the same side of the bed he'd mostly been on when they'd made love. He lifted his feet, sitting there with his back against the headboard, but on top of the covers, a pillow behind him. He was still in his shelter shirt and jeans, but had taken his shoes off. His belt too. He'd placed his gun on the small table beside the bed, seemingly easy enough to grab if he needed it. And Luca certainly hoped he didn't.

Rocky lay down on the floor beside him.

Luca remained standing at the other side, watching him. When he glanced toward her, she shrugged inside. What was the harm of getting back into bed with him? Just being there made her recall their earlier fun. But, that had been before, and it was over.

The night still had some time to go, and her having company in the form of this undercover cop with a gun should allow her to sleep even better than the slight snoozing she'd done after he'd left.

She needed to stay healthy as well as safe, so that was good.

"Are you coming to bed?" he asked, assuming she was still waffling. His deep voice sounded somewhat sleepy. But it remained much too sexy.

What if she said no? Getting in beside him again might make her feel tempted.

She only hoped it would make him feel tempted too... Enough of that.

"Of course." In moments, she'd gotten beneath the covers, beside him, though he remained on top of the blanket. Didn't he want to keep warm even if he didn't sleep?

Well, that was his decision. She suspected he didn't want to get too comfortable, or to fall asleep at all, let alone a deep sleep.

But she regretted that, though they were so near each other, they were far apart, too—both because there were blankets and an emotional distance between them.

He was there to guard. She was there to be guarded, and to sleep. That was the way it was.

She'd already switched off the main bedroom light, but the lamp on the matching table on her side of the bed remained on. As she reached over and shut it off, she realized the room wasn't totally dark.

Mark had turned on the lamp on the table on his side.

She looked over, into his blue eyes. "You need the light on?"

"Just in case I need to look around, that works better."

"Of course."

His protective persona was in charge, as it should be.

Luca settled into the bed, beneath the covers, lying on her side with her head on her pillows, facing away from Mark.

No matter how much she wanted to watch him.

She must have fallen asleep, since sometime later she started awake as she felt a movement at her side. She must have turned over, since now she lay with her back against the mattress. When she looked, Mark was standing.

"Everything okay?" she asked, listening for any sounds, especially from Nicky.

"Fine," he said. "Rocky and I are just going to take a quick walk around the apartment."

"Me too," Luca said right away. "I want to check on Nicky."

She watched Mark, still fully dressed, turn on the hallway light outside the bedrooms and disappear into the living room with Rocky. She carefully opened Nicky's door a little wider and peeked inside.

With the light behind her, she could see that her son was still sound asleep. Her adorable son.

Thank heavens, he was safe—and they had a highly protective man with them who'd make sure things stayed that way.

Luca couldn't help a sigh of relief as she returned to her bedroom.

She had no idea how long Mark might stay out there. Maybe he would spend the rest of the night in the living room or somewhere else in the apartment, keeping watch. Or maybe he'd take his dog and leave, patrolling or returning to his apartment.

Whatever he decided, it would be okay with Luca. She had a sense that he would not do anything that might put her and her son at risk.

He'd do his job.

Although if that was the only reason for him being so protective...

Once again, Luca tried to shut her mind off this time as she settled back into bed. It didn't matter that she'd become so attracted to the man, had even made love with him.

Caring for him would only lead to further hurt, and she'd had enough pain recently to last a lifetime.

And she hoped she would have a nice, long lifetime to come, despite that horrible Morley's threats.

Luca lay on her back, trying not to glance at the open door. She needed to get some sleep. She shouldn't worry about where Mark was, and when, or if, he'd come back to watch over her here.

She couldn't help smiling when he did appear a short while later, Rocky behind him, unleashed. Both came into the bedroom.

She sat up.

"You're still awake?" Mark asked. "You shouldn't worry. Get some sleep."

"I intend to. But—is everything okay out there?"

"As far as I can tell." He sat back on the other side of the bed, twisting his jeans-clad butt on the top of the covers.

"Are you comfortable? Do you want to…well, get undressed? I unfortunately don't have anything you can change into and I don't imagine you want to go get PJs from your apartment, but—"

His look, in the dim lamplight, was one sexy smile that made her insides grow hot. "What, you want me to take my clothes off?"

"I didn't say that exactly but—"

"But yeah." He immediately started doing exactly that. He wore only his underwear as he got beneath the sheet and blanket with her.

In moments, they lay against one another.

Luca felt that her PJs were obstructive against his hard, naked chest. And as they drew even closer together, she felt his erection jutting from those also obstructive boxers.

She reached over despite all her warnings to the contrary and began removing those interfering boxers—even as she felt Mark's hands start to unbutton her pajama top.

"Oh," she breathed as her most sensual parts became hot and moist and needy.

"Yeah, oh," Mark said softly.

And quickly they were both nude.

And touching and kissing and…

Oh, yeah. Making wonderful love once more.

No, that shouldn't have happened. Again.

And yet, afterward, as Mark lay there with Luca snuggled against him, both of them still nude beneath the covers, he was damn glad it had.

Oh, he remained aware of their surroundings even at the best of times, kept his ears open even as his body became engaged. Very engaged. Hot and busy and oh, so active.

After he'd reached his climax—yes, after placing another condom on the appropriate area—he'd lain there breathing hard, feeling Luca against him, her own breathing fast and deep. He was still listening as his sated self began to relax, as if he might soon fall asleep.

That, yes, he might. But not immediately.

"Hey," he said, staying still and feeling Luca's hot and sensual curves remain against him. "And wow."

"Oh, yes. Wow."

Luca, too, sounded satisfied. And happy, he thought. A good thing, since he certainly was.

Despite the fact they shouldn't—

No. No sense going there now. They had done it. He'd wanted to and apparently Luca had too. It was over now. Maybe for the final time. Or not.

"I really…" she said. "I want you to know that, even if we shouldn't—"

"Shh." He looked at her and placed his index finger gently against her lips. "No need to go there now. We did what we did, and I think we both enjoyed it and—"

"I certainly did." She'd been looking at him, too, but now she moved so her head was snuggled against his chest. He liked the feel of her soft, wavy brown hair tickling his skin.

He liked the feel of everything else about her, too, even now when there wasn't so much sensuality but relaxation.

"Good," he said. Then, in case she was wondering, he said, "It's okay to go to sleep now. I will soon, though I won't sleep deeply. I know how to stay somewhat alert even when I'm resting." That was mostly true. When he was on an assignment, he seldom slept deeply.

Of course, he'd never slept with the subject of his assignment before, which Luca had become.

But he trusted himself.

And those outside, who were also law enforcement, watching the place.

Maybe he should get up and walk around the shelter again with Rocky, or at least this apartment. But he heard his dog snoring softly on the floor and was glad the noises Luca and he had made hadn't disturbed his partner and friend.

He decided to remain here. For a short while, he just lay there and listened. Soon, Luca, still in his arms, her warm body soft and still naked, began breathing deeply.

After a short while, Mark did move just a little, pushing his leg over the side of the bed and gently prodding Rocky with his foot so his dog would be the one remaining more alert for now.

It was time, he figured. He allowed himself to drop off to sleep.

He woke now and then, listened to the world around him, including Luca's breathing as she remained against him. Her naked body had begun to arouse him more than once, although he'd forced himself to ignore that.

He figured he slept deeply now and then but had trained himself not to stay that way for long.

And then, as it neared morning, he woke yet again,

Luca still sleeping against him. He ignored his urge to wake her, too, and take advantage of where they were.

That was when he heard something. Nothing worrisome, fortunately.

No, it was a noise from down the hall. A soft voice crying, "Mommy!" Apparently, Nicky had also woken up.

Mark didn't need to wake Luca. She was clearly primed to listen for her son, since she suddenly moved against him, turned and sat up.

She looked back down at him. The lamp was still on, so they could see each other clearly.

"Oh, you're awake?" she asked as she got out of bed.

"Yes. That's not unusual."

"I figured. I did wake up a few times and didn't move, and saw your eyes were open. That made me comfortable enough to fall back asleep after listening and not hearing Nicky."

Interesting. He hadn't realized when that happened. He must have been near sleep himself not to be aware of it.

But since he hadn't sensed danger, he hadn't moved then and must have fallen back to sleep.

He watched as Luca slipped her PJs back on, then opened the partly ajar bedroom door and walked out.

He used the opportunity also to get out of bed and retrieve his phone from his pants pocket. He looked at it. He knew there were no calls since he hadn't turned off the sound. No texts either.

Did that mean all was well? Not necessarily.

But at least nothing had occurred that had made Sherm or Kara or anyone else at the Chance PD decide to get in touch with him. And if they'd called Scott, the shelter's director would undoubtedly have contacted Mark too. Sure, he'd known where Mark was spending the night. Maybe he even suspected that there might be some inappropriate activities going on. But that wouldn't keep him from contacting Mark if there was anything he needed to know.

Like any kind of threat.

As he moved, so did Rocky. "Good boy," Mark said. It was only around 6:00 a.m. and sunrise wasn't officially for another half hour or so, but the sky had been clear, so Mark figured it would be at least somewhat light outside.

And if the sky was still dark, the shelter's lights would remain on anyway.

"Okay, Rocky, let's go out," Mark told his dog. He got dressed and walked down the hall, Rocky behind him. Luca was in the bathroom with Nicky, so he called out, "Rocky and I are taking a quick walk outside. Be back soon."

"Sounds good," Luca called back. "Right, Nicky?"

The little boy yelled, "Right."

Mark figured that response, if nothing else, gave him permission—and he laughed at the thought.

He'd take his K-9 out and check a small part of the grounds to make sure all was still well.

He had left Rocky's leash near the apartment door and grabbed it now, snapping it on, and making sure the door was locked behind them. Luca would undoubtedly let them back in, assuming she remained awake. With Nicky up now, he felt certain she would.

No staffers were in the hallway at this hour. Some might be awake, and a few of those who prepared breakfast might already be in the cafeteria area. He wouldn't stop in to check though. Just a nice, quick outing with Rocky was in his plans for the moment—one in which his dog could do his thing, and Mark could do what was usually on his mind these days: watch and listen for anything out of the ordinary.

They walked down the stairs and soon were out in the center courtyard. The sky was slightly aglow, so the artificial shelter lights were out.

A good time to go for a walk, although they were the only ones out there. Mark would exercise Rocky again later, after breakfast, when some of the staff members were out with other dogs too.

Maybe Luca and Nicky would join him, although having them out and about for long periods of time was probably not a good idea. Luca's enemy wouldn't know where she was within the walls though.

Or, at least, he shouldn't know. But there was no indication that the authorities looking for him outside had any idea about Morley's current location.

Did they?

Probably too early for him to call the station to reach Sherm or Kara for any update they might have.

And so, in the somewhat brisk early morning air, he just walked around.

As he headed back to the apartment building he did see a couple staff members enter the cafeteria, including Sara, the primary cook.

Good. Not that he was hungry yet, but unless he heard

something that made him change his mind, he'd be glad to accompany Luca and Nicky there for breakfast.

He and Rocky walked up the stairs to the fourth floor and Mark knocked on Luca's door. She must have been waiting for him since she answered nearly immediately. "Mark?"

"You got it."

She opened the door and Rocky walked in, followed by Mark, who shut the door and checked to see if it was locked.

"All okay outside?" Luca asked.

"Yep, far as I could tell. And I think breakfast is currently being cooked, so we can head there soon."

"Great. I was just about to get Nicky dressed."

Mark joined them in the boy's bedroom, feeling amazingly happy when Nicky ran over and hugged him. "You're back!"

"Yes, we are. It was time to take Rocky for a walk. Maybe you can go for a walk with us later, after breakfast."

"Yay!" Nicky clapped his hands.

"Time to put your clothes on first," Luca reminded him.

While he did, Mark figured Rocky and he could walk through the small apartment just to confirm all was well there.

As if his thoughts had triggered a reaction, his phone rang just as they walked into the kitchen. "Sit," he told Rocky. His good dog sat and looked up at him with his dark Dobie eyes.

Mark extracted his phone from his pocket. Sherm.

Interesting.

Mark immediately swiped the phone to answer. "Hi, Sherm. What's—"

"Where are you?" the police chief asked.

"In Luca's apartment." Since Sherm's tone sounded curt and upset, Mark didn't attempt any pleasantries like "good morning."

"Good. But here's what you need to do. I've already told Scott, and he should be on his way to Luca's apartment too."

Luca must have heard the phone since she joined him in the kitchen. *Everything okay?* she mouthed. Mark shrugged. He didn't have anything to tell her. Not yet, at least.

She must have realized something was wrong though. She stood on her toes and put her ear near the phone.

Sherm was still talking. "We've gotten a call from Morley. We haven't found him yet, and everything he said could be rubbish. But just in case—"

"What did he say?" Mark demanded.

"He said he's about to attack the shelter, but he's holding off for a little while longer to give Luca time to check her email. That's why I called Scott, since I assume he can give her access."

"Yes. He has before." That was Luca. Her voice was shrill but she hadn't moved away. "Did he say what he emailed me about?"

Mark could guess, but he didn't.

"No, but we do want you to read it."

A knock sounded on the apartment door. "Someone's here," he told Sherm then. "I'll go answer the door. Luca, you stay in here."

"But—"

"Better yet, go into Nicky's bedroom with him." Mark figured she would do that to try to keep her son safe.

"Okay." She looked panicked but obviously wasn't about to object. "But—"

"Go."

She did.

Mark headed to the door, his phone still at his ear. "Who's there?" he asked.

"Scott. Let me in. I'm alone."

That, he might have been forced to say if Morley was with him. But Mark had stuck his gun in his belt beneath his shirt before heading outside with Rocky.

His dog still at his side, always ready to attack if given the order, and his own hand on his gun, Mark opened the door.

Scott came in, shutting it behind him. "I figure you're wondering if I am alone. Well, I am. And, hi, Sherm. I assume that's who you're talking to."

Mark hadn't moved his phone. "Scott said—"

"Hi," Sherm said. "I heard him. Now the two of you need to get busy. Got it?"

"Yeah," Mark said. He hung up the phone. "What's next?" he asked Scott.

"We're going into the office with Luca. She needs to—"

"Check my email," she said, joining the two men near the door.

"Maybe she should do it here," Mark said. "The menace wants her to look at her email and might have a way to get into your office when she—"

"Nah," Scott said. "He'd have no way of getting onto the site to check it out. And he wouldn't know for sure where Luca would be able to get on to a computer anyway, our offices or her apartment or anywhere else, even assuming he knew his way around the shelter, which I doubt. No, my guess is that something he sent in his email is what he wants her to see, wherever it is she looks at it. It'll be bad stuff, undoubtedly, but we need to know what it says."

Mark knew Scott was right. And he would be there, right beside Luca, in the offices or anywhere else when she went online to check out her old email address.

"Let's do it right now," she said. "We need to know what he said. Although…well, I don't want to bring Nicky along, just in case—"

"Nella's in her apartment," Scott interjected. "I'll call and tell her to come watch Nicky, and then we'll head for one of the offices to use a computer."

Made sense to Mark—as much sense as anything else right now.

"That will be great," Luca said, although her tone suggested that nothing could possibly sound great to her at the moment. "Please, ask Nella to come here."

As Scott made the call, Luca looked at Mark in a way that was almost defiant, as if she knew he was against her leaving the apartment now and going to the offices—or anywhere else where she could be in more danger.

"I assume you'll be coming along," she told him.

"You assume right," he said.

Chapter 17

Did she really want to go check her emails? No way. But Luca felt like she had no choice.

Not if she wanted to assist in finding a way to help this shelter remain safe. And its inhabitants, including Nicky and her. And Mark. And even his sweet dog.

While they waited for Nella in the living room, Luca listened to the two men debate whether they should just use one of their cell phones to let her check her email. Their decision, for working together and checking security, as well as tracing Boyle's IP address and location, if he happened to hack into the system, was to get her to a computer in the offices.

That was fine with her.

Especially since she didn't know how much Morley knew about this location. A phone's GPS might make it easier to find her if she used it to respond to his emails.

Right now, even though Morley knew she was in this shelter, she could only assume he wasn't aware of where things were, or where *she* was, inside the tall shelter walls.

Unless he was even craftier than everyone appeared to think.

A knock sounded at the door. "It's Nella," a familiar voice called. Scott was the one to let her in.

Luca led her to the kitchen and showed her some things she could use to play with Nicky. "Mommy has to leave our apartment for a few minutes, honey," she told her son, "but nice Nella is going to stay here with you. You can show her how to play your favorite games. Then we'll go get breakfast."

"Okay, Mommy."

Luca was happy, and a bit relieved, when Nella and Nicky started playing as she left the kitchen.

"You ready?" Scott asked, his tone a bit on edge. He was clearly in a hurry, and Luca figured he expected the worst of her emails.

Well, so did she.

"Yes, let's go." She followed the shelter director out her front door, happy that Mark was behind her. As they headed down the stairs, she noted that he'd left his dog off-leash so Rocky stayed in front of Luca, her guardian behind Scott.

With Mark having her tail… When she had that thought, she kept herself from smiling wistfully. Oh, he had her tail and more.

When they reached the ground floor, they wended their way into the office building, where this time they walked up the steps to the top floor, Rocky behind the humans.

Surprisingly, Scott didn't tell Luca to go into the small front office where she'd been permitted to use a computer before. Instead, they went down the hall to his office.

"You get the front seat," the director told her, motioning for her to sit on his desk chair. He moved his computer to face the side of the desk, and gestured for Mark to reorganize some chairs so they both would face the computer as Luca checked her emails.

Mark told Rocky to lie by the door, then he did as Scott said.

Soon, all of them faced the computer, with Luca closest to it. Scott booted it up and opened the browser where Luca could log into her email.

She wasn't about to reveal how scared she was. She knew these men would do all they could to ensure her safety, and that of everyone else around here, no matter what she saw.

And so she took a deep breath, typed her email address into the screen and entered her password.

She'd gotten some new emails since the last time she'd looked. A couple were from colleagues at her last accounting job. Most she assumed were spam since she didn't always recognize their sources.

But the ones she focused on were those that were clearly from Morley.

There were only a couple.

"Is that from our suspect?" Scott asked from behind her left shoulder, his finger pointing to one of them.

"Yes," she said. "I'll open them chronologically."

That seemed logical to her. But Mark said, "We can check the older one too. But please open the most recent. That'll most likely give us info about what he's up to now."

Or not. But she wasn't going to disagree. These guys were her protectors and more. And she gathered that there was more to Scott than just the director of this shelter, as she'd suspected about Mark before she learned the truth.

"Okay," she agreed.

And so, keeping her hands from shaking as much as she could, she used the mouse to click on the most recent email from Morley Boyle. He used the address of Morley Boyle at a major web service provider. No question about which came from her poor late husband's partner.

The email said:

Hey, Cathleen. I know you've sent the cops to go looking for me, but they haven't found me and they won't. But if you don't get out of there and join me, I'm pretty close to doing what I said before and filling the whole shelter up with tear gas—or something worse. I won't tell you what. So don't worry about today, but you need to walk right out of that place tomorrow and head toward town. I'll be there. I'll find you. And then everyone else there will be safe. So will you, even more than you know, since you'll be with me. Forever.

Luca felt her eyes tear up as she read the message. But she also knew what she had to do. She wouldn't be able to live with herself if anyone was harmed because that psychotic freak got his revenge on the shelter for her not obeying him.

Just in case it contained something that would make her feel better, which she doubted, she closed that one and opened his earlier email.

Hey, Cathleen, it said. I miss you. I'm working on a plan for us to be together. Morley. And that was all. He'd sent it yesterday and must have felt even more frustrated when he hadn't heard back from her.

And so he had worked on his plan...

"Forget that," Mark growled, off to her side, as if he was reading her mind. "Sounds as if he's going to make some kind of move tomorrow, or at least scare you into thinking he is. Well, I'll get in touch again with Sherm and Kara, and I assume you will too, Scott." When Luca looked at him, there was fury emanating from his gaze as he looked at Scott.

"You can be sure of it," the director said. "But they don't know yet—"

"They'd better soon, and definitely before tomorrow," Mark insisted. "I'll be out there with Rocky, too, to make sure the jerk can't get close enough to do anything around here." He looked Luca in the eyes even more closely. "You got that? You're not going to listen to him. You're going to stay safe right here."

"But—" Luca began, hearing herself sob and stopping.

"But nothing."

She wished she could rely on him and the others protecting this place to keep all of them safe. She knew they would all do their damnedest. But she would never forgive herself if something happened to them or to anyone else that was, or even appeared to be, caused by Morley.

And so she turned toward Scott. "I understand, and appreciate, what Mark is saying. But as much as I hate the idea, I really want to do whatever is necessary to make sure Morley is caught before he can do anything horrible. I'd like to tell him I'll do as he says tomorrow, leaving here and walking to town. Could you contact the people you're working with in the local police department and let them know? Maybe they could send undercover cops to keep an eye on me from a distance and catch Morley." She hoped.

But if the man did end up capturing her, maybe that would be enough to keep him from hurting anyone else around here. Even if she became his captive, she'd learn to live with that as long as everyone else—especially Nicky and these men—remained safe.

Or she'd live with it as long as he didn't kill her, as he had George...

"I appreciate your willingness to—" Scott began.

But behind her Mark yelled, "No way!"

She made herself stand and look down at him. "Yes way. It's the only possibility we have of keeping everyone safe, assuming Morley isn't just bluffing and is somewhere around here. He might be just trying to scare me, and therefore the rest of you. We have to call his bluff, if that's what it is, or even let him grab me as long as, hopefully, the local authorities stay near enough to capture him."

"Yeah, right," Mark said. "Hopefully? I like and respect the other cops I work with, but—"

"*But* is right," Scott agreed. "On the other hand, I haven't heard any progress being made in catching the guy."

Luca was looking from one man to the other. She'd already noticed that Scott was a good-looking guy who had a long, handsome face with blue eyes. And Mark? He was even better looking, with thick brows, and blue eyes that were deeper and keener and— Well, she wished she wasn't thinking about any of that now. She had much more important matters to consider.

Like, how she was going to convince these authoritative men, these undercover cops, these dedicated protectors, to let her do what she needed to do so she could protect them, and others, from the horrible man who was after her.

She took a deep breath and said, "Look. You can be sure I hate the idea. But I really don't see another way to deal with this. Unless the cops find Morley by tomorrow, I intend to do what he says and go out there and let the authorities follow me and, if all goes well, capture him then. I'd appreciate you letting your contacts know that's what's going on, and what I'll be doing. Please." She looked first at Scott then turned to look deeply into Mark's eyes.

He looked furious. His teeth must have gnashed together the way she saw his jaw work. And those eyes were flashes of angry light. And yet he still managed to look so handsome... Enough of that.

"Please," she reiterated before either man said anything. Sure, she realized they could do things to prevent her from getting outside the shelter, but hoped they would see reason. "Even cowboys must realize that they sometimes have to lure their prey into circumstances where they can be caught."

That mouth of Mark's moved, almost into a cynical smile. "Yeah, cowboys do what they have to, to get their man."

"I'm not a cowboy," Luca managed to say, "but—"

"Yeah, we get it," Scott said. "And I can't say you're wrong. But here—" He reached into his pocket and pulled out his phone. In a moment, someone answered his call. "Hi, Sherm. Let me tell you what's going on." And he did.

She couldn't help a little sigh of relief at what he said.

Even though she knew she couldn't rely on his promise to keep her safe.

"Hey, yeah. You there, Luca?"

"Yes, and I do intend to go along with Morley's demands, but—"

"But I'm sure you're worried. I can understand it. You can be sure I'll be stepping up our surveillance of the shelter even more, sending more undercover and obvious police cars to keep an eye on things. Scott, you be sure to let me know exactly when Luca goes out the door tomorrow so we can keep her under our observation—her, and her surroundings. And hopefully you've got a phone to give her for GPS tracking, or better yet a wire she can wear so we can trace her. Got it?"

"Yeah, I've got it, and I'll take care of it. Thanks, Sherm."

"No problem." The two men talked a little more, and Mark joined the conversation, asking cogent questions about who and where and how the chief would make sure Luca would remain in their sight. Now, if only he could make good on those promises.

But Luca knew she had to at least attempt to help bring Morley down that way. And she was glad that those in control would be doing their best to keep her safe.

Or at least attempting to.

Soon the conversation was over. The situation, unfortunately, was not.

"Okay," Luca said, attempting to stay in control of herself and the moment, for today, at least. Before she did anything else, she added, "Time for me to send Morley an email to let him know he's won—or at least it should appear that way."

"Good idea," Scott said and moved so she could sit back down at the computer.

Mark remained quiet, but she could feel his eyes boring into her side as she began typing.

Okay, she began the email. I understand what you want, and I will be outside to see you tomorrow at around— She stopped and looked at Scott. "What time do you think I should begin this?"

Scott appeared to ponder for a few seconds then looked at Mark. "Anytime," Mark said. "Like I said, Rocky and I will be going out there, too, to observe— and more, if necessary, though we'll do it in a way that we shouldn't be too obvious to the jerk."

"Oh, but I thought that if I went out there like he said—" Luca began.

But Scott broke in. "Sounds good. We'll let you out a different way, Mark, and we'll rely on the police to do what they need to. So…let's say ten o'clock. It'll be after breakfast and time enough for Sherm to get more of his troops on the road. That okay with you?" he asked Luca.

"Yes, but—"

"Fine. Let Morley know that'll be when you leave, and I'll tell Sherm."

Luca gritted her teeth as she began typing. Ten o'clock was fine.

Mark's interference wasn't. But since she had to go outside, she'd tell Morley that time via this email and then argue with Mark.

Even though she figured objecting would be futile.

She appreciated his help, his protectiveness. She only hoped his being outside at the same time as she was, with his dog, didn't prevent Morley from coming after her—and, hopefully, from getting caught.

After a minute of preparing, sending, and waiting for a response to her email, which didn't come right away, she'd had enough for the moment. Not that she wanted to spend a lot of time thinking about this, but she was certain she would.

For now, though, she wanted to return to Nicky and be with him as long as she could. And hope this day wouldn't be the last time she would be with her son.

"I'm going back to my apartment now to take care of Nicky," she said after again glancing at the computer screen, then rising to look at both men. She logged off her email. She hadn't told them her password and, though she didn't mind these men continuing to look at her email, she didn't want either of them jumping in to say something to Morley that she didn't know about.

"See you both at breakfast then." Scott's tone sounded slightly quizzical. Maybe he figured Luca would, or should, hang out in her apartment. She could feed her son there, after all.

But she didn't intend to let Morley take over her life—at least not for today.

"Yes, Nicky and I will head there soon."

"I'll hang out with you," Mark said.

Luca had an urge to tell him he didn't need to, especially a day before she had to go outside and do—whatever. But, as always, she appreciated his presence, for its protection and more.

"Sounds good," she said.

But nothing sounded good to Mark. Yeah, he'd stay with Luca as much as he could that day, and that night. And even tomorrow.

But he knew that when she went outside as bait to lure Morley into getting caught, if all went well, he wouldn't be able to remain at her side.

He'd be nearby though. As close as possible. Armed, with his K-9, joining in with the cops officially on duty who'd be assigned to take the menacing SOB into custody.

The crafty SOB. He'd undoubtedly know that Luca would have potential protectors around. What was he up to? How was he going to handle that?

Handle her?

Not if Mark could help it. Not in any way.

For now, though, he accompanied Luca back to her apartment, Rocky with them, too, and they soon all went back downstairs to the cafeteria, including Luca's son and Nella.

No issues at breakfast. The crowd of staffers ate happily as usual, thanking Sara and the cooking crew, and laughing and promising all they would do that day was take care of the animals, including training and walking the dogs.

Just like any other day.

The rest of the day seemed the same. Mark did his preferred thing of taking Rocky outside the somewhat secret way after changing his shirt, and walking near, but not too close, to the shelter, keeping an eye on things and making sure no one appeared to be casing the place.

Like maybe Morley, watching to help with whatever his plans were for tomorrow.

Nothing. Although Mark saw other people walking dogs in the park, none looked like Morley's pictures, nor like what he might appear to be in disguise. Not that Mark could be certain. But none of the guys in the area appeared particularly interested in the large, fenced shelter near them.

Cop cars did, though—marked vehicles that patrolled often. There appeared to be a lot of other traffic too. Unmarked cars as well? Maybe.

But did any of them contain Morley? Mark couldn't be sure, but he figured the police who patrolled either obviously or undercover were keeping their eyes on everyone in the area, whether in other vehicles or walking dogs or whatever.

He didn't bother going farther downtown to the police station. He stayed in touch with Sherm and Kara by phone. That would be enough for now.

He took Rocky for a slow walk for just over an hour and decided that was enough for now. They soon returned and wended their way back into the shelter just in time for lunch.

The meal went as well as breakfast, and Mark was glad to take another walk with Rocky, this time inside the shelter while some of the staffers took Nicky for his walk with a few of the dogs being prepared for rehoming.

And then Luca took her son back to their apartment for his nap.

Yes, Mark accompanied them there too.

When Nicky was in bed, Mark sat on Luca's sofa. There was nothing to talk about, really, but he wanted to continue to hang out with her.

To make sure nothing seemed off-kilter anywhere near her, at least for now.

"Are you okay?" she asked as she sat on the other end of the couch.

"Me? Sure."

"You're acting as if…well, never mind. As always, I appreciate you being on alert. And since you disappeared for a while this morning, I assume you sneaked outside and looked around. Everything okay?"

"Yep."

The smile on her beautiful face appeared grim. "For

now. And I do appreciate you not trying to convince me not to go outside tomorrow."

"Oh, I would if I thought you'd pay any attention."

She laughed. And for the rest of the time until Nicky woke up, they turned the television on and watched game shows.

No news, Mark noticed. It was better that way.

Even if there was little possibility Morley would be mentioned. As much as he'd like to hope the jerk would be brought down that day, it was highly unlikely.

When Nicky awoke, it was game time for a while. Then dinner, and Mark was glad when again he sat with them and with the usual staffers, including Bibi, Chessie, Kathy and Leonard.

He also noticed that Scott, sitting with Nella and some of his other staffers, had brought Spike inside. The K-9 remained near their table like Rocky stayed near Mark.

Another short walk around the grounds after dinner. Nicky was taken into the small dog building and allowed to play with some of the occupants, giving commands and laughing when he was obeyed.

All the while, Mark kept watch just in case their enemy had somehow gotten inside, though there was no indication he had.

Finally, it was time to take Nicky upstairs to bed. Mark, with Rocky, prepared to stay the night, although he did take his dog for another couple of short walks around the shelter. He felt in cowboy mode and almost wished he was dressed to look that way. He was in control. He was watchful. He was ready to do anything necessary to accomplish his job, which might not be ranch-related but it was definitely to protect those under his watch.

If only things could remain as safe as they appeared to be tonight.

Mark expected the worst tomorrow, even if he didn't know how he'd fix it. But he would.

The best thing was that he not only got to watch over Luca that night, they wound up making love again. Oh, did they. It was wonderful.

He loved the feel of her. The scent of her, the sound of her soft moans…

If only he could be sure that wouldn't be their final night together.

Darn it, he thought as they finally lay back and prepared to fall asleep. Maybe they wouldn't make love like this again, although he could hope.

But Luca would be fine after tomorrow. He would make sure of it.

Or die trying…

Chapter 18

When Luca woke up the next morning with Mark beside her, she found herself smiling and snuggled back against him as she listened to make sure Nicky wasn't calling out for attention.

Last night had been so wonderful. Again. And—

And then she remembered what today was. That it might be her last day of freedom. Of even being alive.

She bit her lip to prevent herself from crying out. But she must have made some noise, stirred somehow, since Mark said softly, "You're awake?"

"Yes." She hated the cracking tone of her voice. She might as well act normal—as long as she could.

"We should get up then," he said, though he put his strong, warm arms around her, and it was all she could do to avoid sobbing.

No. That wasn't the way she would handle this. She would be strong. She might be relying on others to ultimately save her, but she would do all she could to bring Morley down, to prevent him from harming others and, preferably, her too.

She had the urge to reach down and touch Mark and make love one more time. But no, she had to check on her son. To get this day started.

To prepare herself as much as possible for what was going to occur at ten o'clock.

"You can use the bathroom first while I check on Nicky," she said, realizing that sounded like things were normal.

"Fine. I'll be quick." As she got up, she couldn't help watching Mark and his nude, hard, amazing body as he walked to the bathroom. She absorbed the view as well as she could.

This could be the last time she would see him naked.

Enough. She walked to the closet, pulled out her robe and put it on. Then she opened the door and went down the hall.

Nicky was still asleep. She needed to wake him, though, so she called softly, "Nicky? Time to get up."

He opened his eyes, but he took his time getting out of bed.

"Let's go brush your teeth," she said, since she no longer heard the water running in the bathroom.

"Okay, Mommy."

She knew this time Nicky would know Mark stayed the night, but that was okay. She hurried him to the bathroom.

After his face washing and teeth brushing, she helped

him get dressed, then left him in the kitchen. Mark and Rocky weren't there, so she figured they'd gone for their early walk.

It was her turn to shower and dress and start heading for the cafeteria with her son.

Mark met them partway and walked with them, Rocky alongside him. Sweet, but she surely didn't need his protection at the moment.

And after ten o'clock… Well, she wouldn't think about that now.

Breakfast seemed like it always was, or at least how it was in the few days they'd been there.

Afterward too. She didn't imagine any of the staff members knew what she was about to face, but several seemed glad to take charge of Nicky again and help him walk with dogs in the somewhat brisk outside air. Especially Chessie, who was walking Spike, the German shepherd, the young staffer, Leonard, who had Jade the Great Dane with him, the senior Augie with small, white Oodles, and Kathy with Mocha.

Luca observed them all, especially when one held out a leash to Nicky to let him lead the dog along the central pathway of the shelter.

"Come with us, Nicky," older, wiser and clearly caring Kathy said as she gave him Mocha's leash.

"Yeah!" Nicky said as he took it.

Luca loved watching them.

And hoped this wouldn't be the last time.

But at least Nicky was in good company, and she was particularly glad when Nella joined them. That shelter manager had done a wonderful job watching over her son at various times, and she would again now.

She took Nella aside briefly. She figured Scott's girlfriend would know, or learn, what was going on, so she handed her the information she'd written down on how to contact her parents, if it became necessary. They had a signed copy of her will. She'd seen an attorney and had it created when Morley had begun threatening her...

"It contains my wishes about further care of Nicky—Davey. My family will have the right to take him in."

"I understand," Nella said. "But hopefully it's being overly cautious to worry about that now."

"Hopefully," Luca agreed...but she couldn't be sure.

Now, as the time approached ten o'clock, Luca hoped Nella would continue to take care of Nicky. Maybe for a very long time—

No. Pessimism wouldn't help her get through this.

And somehow, she would.

"Hey," came a voice from behind her on the path.

Startled, Luca jumped—and felt a hand on her shoulder. A caring hand.

She wasn't surprised, especially after the deep sound of that voice, to see it was Mark.

"You okay?" he asked.

"You tell me." She tried to sound amused but realized she hadn't hidden her inner angst.

"You will be." He looked down at her with those blue eyes both compassionate and determined, and for a moment, at least, she felt better.

She walked with Rocky and Mark a short while, staying behind Nicky, Kathy and Mocha. She forced herself not to look at her wristwatch, although she knew ten o'clock was drawing even closer.

But she didn't have to worry about being late. Mark stopped walking at the same time they were approached by Scott.

The shelter director also appeared concerned as he told her, "It's quarter to ten. If you don't want to go outside, I'll let the police chief know and—"

"I'm going out." Luca knew her voice quivered, even as she tried to state her intention firmly.

"All right then. I unfortunately don't have a wire I can attach and we don't have time for me to wait to get one, but here's a cell phone, with GPS." He handed one to her, and she stuffed it deep inside her pants pocket. "I'll walk you to the shelter entrance and call Chief Shermovski." He aimed a glance toward Mark.

"Make sure Sherm keeps us informed," Mark said. "Rocky and I will be taking a walk now, too, though we're leaving through a different door."

Luca wasn't surprised. She felt a tiny bit relieved, although she knew Mark being somewhere outside the shelter, keeping an eye on her, wouldn't guarantee her safety, especially since he wouldn't be able to stay near her if there was any hope at all that Morley would come close to her and potentially be caught by the police.

"Sounds good," was all she said, although it didn't really sound very good.

Soon, Scott and she arrived at the building that contained the hallway with the vet clinic and rooms where new potential shelter staffers were interviewed, and where people coming in to possibly adopt pets housed at the shelter could meet their potential new family members. They quickly reached the door at the end with the waiting room on the other side.

As Scott, continuing to use his key card at all the doors, ushered her into that room, he looked down at her in obvious concern. "You can still change your mind."

"I know," she said. "But I won't." How could she, with him and everyone else in this shelter, including its animals—and Mark and Rocky, and most especially Nicky—in peril?

And she knew the authorities, thanks to Scott, would be keeping track of her, using the GPS on the cell phone she'd been given.

"Okay then." They reached the door to the outside, and again Scott swiped his key card. And then he pulled the door open. "I'm calling Sherm now. I'm sure there are already patrols around, but he needs to know you're outside." He seemed to hesitate before saying, "Please be careful."

"I will," Luca said as forcefully as she could muster. And she would, as much as she could.

But she almost stumbled as she exited and began looking around the street, and the park across from it, for the danger she knew she faced.

It all appeared as it had last time she'd seen it, when she'd come inside for the protection of this shelter.

The protection that was no longer surrounding her.

But she wouldn't cry. Instead, she took a bold step forward. She knew the general direction of downtown Chance from here. As had been discussed with her, that was where she would head.

All the while keeping watch around her. Being careful, as she'd assured Scott, rightly or wrongly.

And hoping she survived—and that Morley at last was caught.

There wasn't a lot of traffic around. Not even any police cars, at least not then. She couldn't help attempting to see the drivers of the few cars, SUVs and even trucks that went by, but she wasn't able to make out many faces, and none she saw appeared to be Morley.

Even so, some, at least, could be undercover cops out here to keep an eye on the shelter and everyone around it. She hoped.

As she got ready to cross the street, a police car drove by slowly, and the officers inside appeared to be observing the outside of the shelter.

Her too? Could be. Maybe they'd been told what was going on, and to look out for her. Maybe they'd been given the information to track the cell phone she now had.

She hoped. And since the driver waved briefly at her, she assumed that could be the case.

She got across the street and looked toward the park. She liked walking in parks, especially with Nicky. But she might not be visible from the road, which could be a bad thing if that was where Morley was waiting for her.

No, she decided to stay on the sidewalk, not close to the curb, and walk around the area, heading ultimately in the direction of town.

And continuing to watch for Morley.

She also watched for Mark and Rocky, since they were outside the shelter now, keeping an eye on her.

She didn't see them though. That was probably by design. If Mark was out there, he'd want to observe her surroundings but not be too obvious.

Well, she knew she couldn't rely on him to keep her safe, despite his remaining her protector. Sweet guy. But only human, even with his K-9 sidekick along.

And her? Okay, yes, she remained nervous. Anticipated the worst, even though she hoped nothing bad happened.

Meanwhile, she took a deep breath and did what she could to bolster her own courage.

Okay Morley, she thought. *I did what you said. I'm out here. Now come and get me.*

But preferably only when there were skilled, trained, alert and accomplished police officers around who'd grab him first.

For now, she decided she wouldn't allow herself to look as nervous as she was. She lifted her chin and, though walking very fast didn't seem like a good idea, she began strutting forward, hoping she appeared confident.

More confident than she was…

There she was, across the street.

Mark had done his usual thing of sneaking out of the shelter with Rocky, then easing their way along as if they were ordinary civilians just taking a walk. But he didn't maneuver across the street and into the park, to hide them, as usual, as they walked toward the police station.

Nor did he get close to Luca and make them more

obvious if that jerk, Morley, happened to be right here—among both the undercover and obvious authorities patrolling.

The morning air was warm, the sounds of birds, voices and traffic minimal, and apparently the smells in the area weren't very exciting, considering how Rocky didn't seem too inclined to keep his nose in the air or to sniff the sidewalk beneath them.

And so they walked. Slowly.

With Mark keeping an eye on Luca a short distance from them, but far enough away to be on her own.

Potentially in danger, and too far for him to protect her.

But at least he would watch her. Keep in touch with Sherm and Kara. He called Kara as soon as he'd gotten outside the shelter, since Sherm had indicated she was to be his primary contact that day.

Kara said that both she and Sherm were among the drivers in the area, a potentially good thing, Mark figured. But would they be any more helpful in catching their suspect?

"Thanks, Kara," he said nevertheless, and told her he had nothing to report.

He did, however, have the information from the cell phone Luca had been given, so if she somehow got out of sight, he'd be able to track the GPS.

Luca wasn't far away, though there was now a street between them. He and Rocky would soon cross it, as long as they didn't get too close to her.

She seemed to glance his way, then draw her gaze slowly away, as if he was just some guy, a stranger, walking his dog, along with several others around there, mostly on her side of the street where the park was.

Did his being there help her state of mind? Or was she pretending to be someone taking a walk for enjoyment, picking up her pace, her chin raised as if she hadn't a care in the world?

It didn't matter why she'd started acting that way, as if the fear she'd expressed while telling those in charge at the shelter that she was coming out here no matter what didn't really exist.

Oh, she was one hell of a woman in so many ways. Mark's body reacted as he recalled last night, as if it was ever far from his mind. She was sexy. Oh, yeah.

And she was a wonderful mom to her little Nicky, putting his enjoyment, and his safety, well above her own.

Everyone else's safety too. She was brave, facing whatever danger there might be out here from Morley no matter what, doing what she could to protect the other people inside the shelter.

Even him.

He had the urge to hurry to her side, to hug her and shield her from the world as well as he could with his body—and the weapon stuck into his belt.

Oh, yeah, his cowboy persona was doing its best to come out and show the world who he was—and to be used to do whatever he had to, to protect that courageous, beautiful, amazing woman he was keeping his eyes on.

She was nearing the corner across the street. He slowed down, pulling Rocky's leash gently, while he observed which way Luca was traveling. She stayed on the same block, on the other side of that portion of the park.

He headed that way too.

Going slowly, attempting to appear nonchalant, he stepped to the curb and looked at the vehicles going both directions. Not too many, and there was a break during which he was able to cross the street with Rocky. On the other side, he pretended to check his watch, as if determining how much more time he had for his walk, and then he started again in the direction Luca had gone.

At the corner, he and Rocky turned in the same way she had.

About the same amount of traffic went this way, more cars and SUVs and, yes, a couple of police cars.

He couldn't help looking into them. He recognized one of the drivers but not the other, and it wasn't Kara or Sherm.

He didn't wave, and neither did his fellow Chance PD officer who was in uniform.

Mark continued walking slowly with Rocky. No one who observed them would imagine this was some kind of exercise power walk. That was fine.

But he did go fast enough to make certain to keep Luca in view. She'd slowed a bit, and her gait was now similar, also not attempting to get any exercise value out of this.

Any value? Like luring Morley closer?

Mark figured at least some of the unmarked cars were driven by undercover cops. One way or another, if Morley—

Wait! One of the Chance PD cars passed him and

stopped beside Luca. She was still walking, but the cop driver got out.

Had he heard of some trouble nearby? Was he warning her?

Oh, no. Just the opposite. He grabbed her arm and pulled her toward the police vehicle. She screamed.

"Rocky, come," Mark shouted, and he and his dog ran toward where the clash was occurring.

Could he get there in time to save her?

He had to.

Chapter 19

As the cop grabbed her, Luca immediately recognized Morley despite the police cap on his head with the brim pulled down to obscure the upper part of his face.

Her husband's former partner.

He had never seemed especially good-looking to Luca, nor particularly ugly. But at the moment, with his brown eyes glaring from beneath the brim, and his vicious, teeth-baring scowl, he appeared horrible.

Repellant.

Frightening.

Though she fought him, he was too strong. He quickly shoved her into the passenger seat of the car, quickly snapping several long zip ties around her wrists and hands, securing them together and fastening her to the seat. He then shoved something that felt like a rag into her mouth so she couldn't scream again.

Had anyone seen what was going on?

Where were the other police around here who were supposed to be protecting her?

Surprisingly, the uniform Morley wore had a Chance Police Department insignia. The car he dragged her into looked just like the other cop cars on the street, apparently one owned by the local police department too.

How had he managed that?

Not that she could ask with the gag thrust deep into her mouth.

He slammed the door closed beside her and in moments was in the driver's seat. He locked the doors and began driving away.

Was this it? Was she going to die?

Not if she could help it. But what could she do, while bound and gagged like this?

He had to stop somewhere, she figured. And unless he shot her as she sat there, surely she would have some opportunity to save herself.

She knew she was shaking. She made herself ponder what to do next. Could she get him to remove the gag so she could talk to him? Not that she was likely to convince him to let her go.

"At least you did as you said and came outside of the shelter," Morley said from beside her. His voice was an angry snarl, even as he said something slightly approving of her. "But I shouldn't have had to do this. You shouldn't have run away, come to this place where it was so hard to get in touch with you, let alone see you."

She made a noise in her throat as if responding to him, even as she glanced out the window. They weren't going very fast. There were cars around them. But still not a lot.

She felt sure he'd be able to get around them.

But had anyone seen what happened? The local police were supposed to be keeping an eye on her. Attempting to nab Morley. Or so she'd believed.

They'd failed so far. Maybe, even if they'd noticed, they hadn't wanted to pull him over, for her protection. If he was surrounded, he might kill her.

Although would he use her as a hostage to gain his own release?

How would she know?

She almost laughed inside. At the moment, she didn't know anything except that she was in big trouble. But she'd come out here, as ordered. Hopefully, Morley would leave the shelter and its inhabitants alone.

No matter what he did to her.

And that was why she had complied. But she still hoped to survive.

She believed Mark was following her, with Rocky. But now that she was in a car, he wouldn't be able to catch up with her.

Well, she had to do something to save herself. And so she started trying to talk despite the gag in her mouth.

The noise she made wasn't comprehensible even to her. But it at least got his attention as he continued to drive forward.

"What is it, Cathleen?" He only knew her by her real name. But she still thought of herself as Luca. "Don't you know how much I hate doing this? But it's the only way we can be together right now."

She made another noise, hoping it sounded sad. She had to play along with him, or at least make him think so.

"I'll take that out next time we stop. If I yank it while I'm driving, it may hurt you and I could lose control of the car. So for now…"

He'd been peering through the windshield, but quickly glanced in the rearview mirror. He didn't appear concerned about anything he saw, since he kept driving.

That worried Luca more. With luck, they were being followed surreptitiously, with no pursuing authority in clear view.

But maybe there wasn't anybody. Although she had seen police cars before. Where were they now?

And wasn't someone still monitoring her GPS? She still felt the phone in her pocket. Fortunately, Morley hadn't looked for one.

"Here's what you need to know. Or maybe you already do. I've always cared about you, Cathleen, and thought you cared about me too." He aimed a glance at her, and she made herself nod. "Really? I'm so glad. You know that was why I decided to remove George from your life, to free you so you and I could be together."

Oh, Lord. She'd suspected that before, and now he'd admitted it. If only she'd understood then, while George had still been with them, what Morley's friendliness had really meant.

If only she could have prevented him from killing George. She'd still cared about her husband, even though their relationship had soured.

But she never would have killed him. And she certainly didn't want anything to do with the man who had murdered him.

Right now, maybe it was a good thing she couldn't speak. She didn't know what she would say to this murderous lunatic.

Especially if she couldn't also attack him in some way and get her freedom back.

"But even after George was out of your life, you didn't seem interested in spending time with me." Morley's voice turned hard again, and he leveled a furious glare as he glanced at her. Talk about the possibility of losing control of the car. He seemed to be losing control of himself first.

If only she could talk and at least ask him to pull over so they could continue this discussion.

This currently one-sided discussion.

She attempted to make her wordless voice sound apologetic as she uttered her next sounds.

He must have gotten it since he looked away as he continued driving.

"And then you disappeared. I had to find you. That's why I sent you threatening emails. And when you didn't respond to them right away…well, I'm really glad I learned where you were. And though I didn't like threatening you or anyone else, here we are." His voice rose and sounded strangely happy. "You're with me now. I'm going to show you how much I care for you so you'll finally care for me even more. We can get your little son to join us soon."

Luca's heart sank. No. He couldn't have Nicky. No way.

She was shocked when Morley suddenly pulled over

to the curb and stopped. He kept the engine running, his foot on the brake, but he reached over and removed the gag.

"Now, I want to hear what you have to say."

He left her bound to the seat though.

She felt certain that, if she said anything he didn't like, she wouldn't like the consequences.

Assuming she even survived.

Mark hadn't waited. Running, with Rocky beside him, he'd intended to plant himself in front of the car Luca had been thrown into and to stop the driver, presumably Morley, from driving off with her.

But though he hadn't been far away, and he'd watched Luca be bound and gagged, he and Rocky hadn't gotten there fast enough, damn it. The car had taken off, going through the nearest intersection. He didn't know if Morley had looked back and seen Mark while he was out of the car. Best he could tell, the guy was now watching Luca and the road and not necessarily anyone around them.

Not that it mattered.

What the hell was he going to do? He immediately decided to pull over one of the marked cars and make certain the cops inside knew what had happened, if they hadn't seen it.

They had to follow Morley. Get him blocked off and stopped.

But would that cause him to kill his captive?

For now, Mark followed as best he could along the sidewalk after crossing the street in the direction the car had gone, Rocky running beside him. His cowboy instincts made him wish he was riding a horse, avoiding all the cars that could get in his way.

But he had to deal with the situation as it was. How could he get one of the police vehicles to stop and pick him up?

As if someone was reading his mind, one of those cars pulled up and stopped beside him. Assistant Police Chief Kara rolled down the automatic window on the passenger side, nearest the sidewalk. "I saw what happened. Get in."

Good. At least there was a chance.

He did what she said, opening the back door of the car, shooing Rocky inside and then entering himself. A uniformed officer was driving. His name badge ID'd him as Ricker.

"Hi," Mark said, leaning forward on the back seat. "Thanks. Now, what are we going to do?"

"Stop him," Kara said. "Hopefully get Luca out safely. I've got other cars ahead of him ready to block him on the road. But with a suspect as malicious and determined as that, I'm afraid he'll harm her before we can prevent it." She paused. "He stole that patrol car, of course. The officers in it were stopped at a stop sign at an intersection a few miles away from the area we were officially patrolling. He aimed his gun at them. They tried to shoot him first, but as soon as they lowered the driver's window, he shot the closest officer. Not dead, fortunately, but both of them wound up exiting the car and he knocked them unconscious with the butt of his gun. Then he removed the jacket and cap of one of them and apparently put them on."

"Anyone who saw him driving that car afterward would assume he was just a regular local cop on patrol, like all the others." Mark was fuming but it unfortunately made sense.

And now, Luca, the woman he was supposed to be protecting—the woman he now realized he had come to really care about, maybe even love, in the short time he'd known her—was in terrible danger.

She might not get out of this alive. If he'd remained closer to her—

No. Blaming himself now wouldn't help. But he had to rescue her before she was physically harmed.

"Let's go," he said, and they did.

Could they spot the right police car among the others? It seemed like the whole fleet was around here, obviously alerted to what was going on. And Kara would know the official ID number of the stolen cop car.

There were civilian vehicles in the area, too, and some were probably unmarked cars staffed by undercover cops.

Oh, yes, the likelihood that there was a whole troop of cops around to bring down Morley was encouraging.

They'd probably succeed.

But without Luca getting hurt?

Mark would do his damnedest to ensure she remained okay. They'd pulled up to the rear of a lot of stopped vehicles on the road.

"Hey," Kara said. "Looks like we've got him trapped." She got on her phone and soon was talking to one of those officers, presumably in one of the cars nearest the one in question. Mark could hear some of what was going on.

"Yeah," said a low and somewhat muffled voice that he could make out nonetheless. "We've got him boxed in. We'll be using a speaker to tell him to exit his vehicle slowly, hands up and all."

As if he'd obey. But since they were stopped, Mark knew what he had to do.

After requesting that Kara unlock the back door beside him which had automatically locked, he opened it and jumped out, holding Rocky's leash. His Doberman K-9 leapt down beside him. "Come on, boy," Mark said.

Bending over to be a bit less visible, Mark maneuvered his way along the road among the cars there, Rocky with him, until they were a couple of cars behind the subject vehicle.

By then, one of the cops in the car blocking Morley's had gotten out and was facing it, a bullhorn in his hand. Mark assumed the officer was wearing more PPE—personal protective equipment—than the vest and face mask he wore since he was easily within Morley's line of fire.

The speaker blared. "Get out of the car!"

Nothing from Morley.

"You can't get away, so get out and let's end this safely. Let your hostage go now!"

Still nothing.

Mark continued forward, ready to break open the passenger window near Luca with the butt of his gun, since the other windows were not as strong as the bulletproof windshield, though he'd have to be careful she wasn't hit by much, if any, glass. Hopefully, when he started, Morley's attention would still be occupied by the cop with the speaker.

Mark was ready to do anything he had to do to save Luca.

And then—the driver's door opened.

Somehow, Morley shoved Luca out from on top of him, then followed her out the door with a gun to her head. He stood there that way, looking around from one cop car to another.

"Okay, I'm out!" he shouted. "Yeah, let's end this safely. Just let me go, and I'll walk out of this area with Ms. Cathleen, here, and won't hurt her. But if you try to stop me, or to hurt me, you'll have her death on your consciences."

Damn. Not a surprise, but this standoff wasn't about to go anywhere.

Not without Mark's intervention.

He continued walking with Rocky, his gun in his hand at his side. Fortunately, no one else was on the sidewalk. He saw no civilians around, so no one else would get hurt.

He hoped no one did, especially not the subject of his protection.

At least Morley was facing the other way, but he could turn at any moment, Luca under his control. And he could shoot her or use her as a shield as he fired at Mark.

Damn. At least he was getting closer now.

Time to act.

"Rocky, attack," he said loud enough for his K-9 to hear but hopefully Morley wouldn't.

Didn't matter. His wonderful dog obeyed the command as usual. In moments, the Dobie ran forward and leapt at the man holding Luca, the only person obvious for the dog to see and attack.

"Hey!" Morley yelled as he was shoved to the ground by the fast, soaring K-9. He didn't let go of Luca, who screamed as she, too, fell down, but Rocky knew who his quarry was. He grabbed Morley's right arm with his teeth, and Luca, crying but loose now, was able to move away.

But that damn gun was still in Morley's hand. Rocky's vicious bite hadn't made him drop it. As he aimed toward Luca and attempted to pull the trigger, Mark reached him and put the barrel of his own weapon against the perp's head.

"Drop it!" he shouted.

"Get this damn dog off me," Morley yelled in return.

But he did lower his weapon as he continued unsuccessfully to try to fight off Rocky.

Mark quickly kicked the gun out of the way then said, "Rocky, release."

Of course, Rocky did as he was told.

By then, other cops had joined them and Mark was able to stop aiming his weapon at Morley as he was taken into custody. He heard the familiar words of the Miranda rights from Kara, who, expectedly, was in charge.

"Morley Boyle, you are under arrest. You have the right to remain silent. Anything you say can and will be used against you in a court of law. You have a right to an attorney. If you cannot afford an attorney, one will be appointed for you."

Only then did Mark kneel and gently grab Luca, who'd remained on the ground, crying softly as she lay there. But she turned around and was looking at him.

"You okay?" he asked softly as he pulled her closer.

"I am now." She started to rise, and he helped her. Her hands were bound in zip ties, and he'd get them off her in a moment.

For now, she turned and glanced down at Rocky, who stood near them, tail wagging. "Thank you, Rocky," she said.

She turned again, looking up into Mark's eyes. Inappropriate, yes, but he took her into his arms.

"And thank you, Mark," she said, and kissed him.

Chapter 20

It was finally over, Luca thought. Except for the waning fear and other emotions that remained within her.

But she was at the Chance police station now. She had been driven there, along with Mark and dear, life-saving Rocky in the back seat, and another cop driving as she sat in the front passenger seat, her hands unbound. Assistant Police Chief Kara requested that she come and give a statement about what happened.

She was in Kara's office. It was a large office, with a very neat and highly professional-looking desk that had a stack of folders on it, and a computer was on a table at the side of her chair. Not that Luca really knew what an assistant police chief's office looked like. But she felt comfortable there.

Even when she was told to sit on one of the black

chairs facing the desk, with Mark taking a seat beside her, Rocky on the floor near him, and Kara, efficient-looking in her uniform and pretty, at the other side of the desk.

And then the chief, Shermovski, joined them too.

"So," Kara said, "tell us what happened."

Luca did so, choking up at times as she gave her statement about everything that had happened that morning since she walked out of the shelter.

She knew she sounded awful as she spoke, even cried, but she continued, answering questions from the chief and assistant chief. She knew what she said was being recorded, and both took notes too.

Soon, they were finished. "Thanks so much," older, also uniformed Sherm said as they all stood and moved toward the office door. "We'll be in touch if there are more questions. And we'll appreciate your cooperation as we investigate the case further, then prosecute Mr. Boyle for what he's done here. Plus, he'll also be subject to prosecution in Cranstone for the murder of your husband. I will stay in close contact with the authorities there to keep them informed about the progress here before passing him into their custody."

"You shouldn't have to worry about seeing him again, except in court," Kara assured her.

"Thank heavens." Luca couldn't help sighing.

"But please don't talk about what happened, or what we discussed here, except when it's absolutely necessary," Sherm said. "We don't want anything to undermine our prosecution."

"Got it," Luca said.

"But do let us know if we can help you get any medical attention you need," Kara added, "or a referral to a lawyer since you will need to testify about all this in court."

"Thanks," Luca said. "I'm fine for right now but I'll let you know if I need anything more."

And then, apparently, this part was over too.

"I'll drive you back to the shelter," Mark said.

"Thanks."

Luca remained quiet in the police car Mark currently drove. Yes, he was an officer with the Chance PD and wasn't hiding it now, at least not from her. But she assumed he would soon go back undercover at the shelter.

She couldn't wait to see Nicky again. But what would come next in their lives? They wouldn't need to stay in protective custody at the shelter.

Where would they go? If they left, she would of course return to testify at Morley's trial, whenever that happened. But till then…?

She couldn't help glancing at Mark as she considered that. He had been such a wonderful part of her life over the past few days of worry and terror.

But soon he would no longer be in her life.

Now that she and Nicky were safe—hey. They wouldn't be in protective custody much longer. They could resume their former lives…somehow.

"You know what?" she said to Mark. "I won't be Luca much longer. I'll be Cathleen again, and Nicky will be Davey."

"Makes sense to me," he said with a smile, flashing a really great blue-eyed glance toward her as he pulled into a parking spot a couple blocks from the shelter.

"Not until we leave the shelter though," she added. "It would be too confusing."

"Right. But I'll have fun thinking of you as Cathleen and Davey soon."

Things were changing, and Mark was okay with her going back to her old life.

That was as it should be.

He'd be thinking of her then—maybe. But they wouldn't be together.

And that made her feel sad.

Mark was proud he and Rocky had helped get Luca out of that horrible predicament safely. No, Cathleen—soon. But not yet.

He wasn't at all surprised that, now that she didn't need to be in the protective custody of Chance Animal Shelter, she would be taking back her real name. Her son too. There was no reason for them to remain here, even in this area, although he recognized she'd need to return briefly when Morley was prosecuted at trial.

He assumed she and Nicky—Davey?—would return to their old home in Cranstone, California, and resume their former lives without any threats looming over them.

"So," he said, "I imagine your time here for the rest of today, and maybe even tomorrow, will be spent saying goodbye. Maybe you can even let the staff members know a little of what happened so they can believe that they, too, might eventually get beyond the dangers that drove them to stay in this protective shelter."

"I don't think, from what Sherm and Kara told me, that I should talk too much about it, at least not until

Morley is convicted. But I guess I can say something about it without being specific."

"Exactly."

They both got out of the vehicle along with his dog. Another police car had been close behind them and one of the officers exited that car and settled into the driver's seat to drive their vehicle back to town. No one inside the shelter would have seen the car they'd arrived in.

They walked the short distance to the outer door of the shelter's reception area, and Mark used his key card to let them in.

He'd called before they'd left the station, while Luca was still talking with Sherm and Kara, to let Scott know what had happened.

Time passed since the ordeal began that morning, and it was nearing dinnertime. First thing, though, he and Rocky accompanied Luca down the walkway inside the shelter. They found Nicky alongside the small dog building, working with Chessie, who had Lallie the spaniel with her, and Leonard with Mocha. The boy's hand was in the air and he was telling Lallie to "Sit!" A few other staffers walked the usual dogs along the walkway near them, but Luca dashed to her son as soon as she saw him.

"Mommy!" Nicky yelled and ran to her too. They hugged, and Mark wished he could join them, as inappropriate as that was.

But he wouldn't have an opportunity to hug either of them ever again very soon...

Scott and Nella hurried up to them then.

"I'm so glad you're okay," Nella said, and she joined in the hug fest.

Scott said to Mark, "I want to hear everything that happened. But right now, we're planning a little celebration at dinner."

That occurred just a short while later.

After nearly everyone had entered the cafeteria and gotten their food, Scott stood at the end of the table occupied by Nella and others, as well as Mark, Luca and Nicky—still their names for now.

Scott raised his water glass in a toast. "Everyone, we have some good news. The problems Luca had that brought her here were resolved today, and now she and Nicky will soon be going back to their home. Here's to a wonderful new life for them." He lifted the glass further then took a drink.

Everyone at the nearly filled tables did the same thing, and many cheered and clapped. "Hear, hear!" some shouted.

"Tell us all about it," Bibi yelled, grinning enough that the gap between her front teeth was more than obvious.

Luca, sitting beside Mark, looked at him with a nervous expression, but she did stand. "I think some of you know I...well, I walked out of the shelter earlier today because of a difficult situation and—"

"Someone was threatening you, right?" Kathy called out.

Luca took a deep breath and nodded. "Yes. But thanks to the Chance Police Department, as well as our wonderful staff member Mark and his dog, Rocky, I'm okay and the situation was handled, well enough that Nicky and I are no longer under threat. Unfortunately, I can't say any more about it."

"Someone's going to prison, right?" Leonard, at the table near them, blurted.

Luca only smiled.

"And Mark. Are you actually a cop?" Leonard asked.

"I'm just someone who tries to help if someone I care about is in trouble," he said. "Fortunately, I— Well, I wasn't supposed to, but I was outside the shelter walking Rocky when all this occurred."

"Sure," Leonard said. His young face appeared amused, but he didn't push any further.

And Mark wondered if everyone now suspected, or knew, his real background.

That led him to another thought... Well, he would have to ponder it further.

He wondered if he would get to see Luca and Nicky after dinner. He no longer had to stay in their apartment to protect them. But if he could keep them company just one more night...

A while later, after they finished eating and visited some of the dogs again, Luca turned to him and said, "I need to get Nicky to bed now. And I know you don't have to hang out with us anymore. But if you'd like to come visit...and maybe stay with me this last time... Well, I'd really like that."

"Count on it," he said.

And he did. They had quite a wonderful night, as far as he was concerned. Sex? Oh, yeah. Definitely lovemaking, as quietly as they could manage it with Nicky asleep in the next room.

Lovemaking he'd remember forever.

Even so, he had an idea and he would follow through with it as much as possible the next day.

* * *

Morning arrived much too soon, Luca thought the next day. In some ways.

But, hey, she and Nicky were about to start a whole new chapter in their lives. One in which they wouldn't be in danger, needing to stay in this shelter for protection.

Though she wasn't certain what would actually come next. She could go home to her parents. Or return to Cranstone. Or—well, she would need to figure it out.

But without Mark's input or opinion, apparently.

He gave her a kiss on the forehead before she went to wake Nicky and told her that Rocky and he were going for an early walk outside. That he'd hopefully see her later that day, before she left the shelter. She'd be here for a while, figuring out where to go and getting Scott's advice, right?

"Yes," she told Mark, feeling both puzzled and hurt. She would look forward to seeing him later—probably for the last time. But he was leaving now, so she wouldn't be able to spend her last hours here with him.

Well, okay, she told herself after Mark left. She would just have as great a time here with Nicky as she could. She'd make some calls outside, Scott permitting, and try to determine where she and her son would go from here to figure out what was next.

Breakfast was amazing, with so many staffers coming over and professing how much they'd enjoyed having her, and especially her little boy, among them.

Afterward, Nicky was shown another fantastic time exercising and training several dogs. Luca knew she would have to find a way to make sure Nicky had at least one, and maybe more, dogs in his life. They could volunteer at a shelter near wherever they wound up, she hoped.

Then Chessie took over watching Nicky while Luca went into Scott's office and talked to him about her future possibilities. He told her he wasn't kicking her out, so she could stay another day or two if she wanted.

"Thanks," she said. "I may just do that. But I'll have to contact some people outside so I'll know where we should end up at first."

And if she stayed another night or two, she'd get to see Mark again. A good idea? Maybe not. But surely it wouldn't hurt.

Mark. Where was he? It was getting near lunchtime. He was definitely taking a long walk with Rocky. She knew he didn't want to be seen outside. He needed to be here for the undercover work he'd been assigned. She knew that, but the others didn't. Did they?

Using one of the shelter phones, Luca made a few calls, including to her former boss at the financial firm in Cranstone where she'd worked as an accountant.

Harry sounded happy to hear from her, said yes, they could probably find a position for her if she came back, which made her smile.

Good. She had a possibility that could work.

And she could consider other possibilities before deciding, though she didn't know what yet.

Maybe they should head back to Cranstone tomorrow.

At least that would give her one more night here at

the shelter. With Mark? She could hope so. But where was he?

All sorts of thoughts came to her as she watched some of the regular staffers work with Nicky. There were even more of them than usual, playing and showing him new tricks and seeming to have a good time with him.

Maybe trying their hardest because they wouldn't see him anymore.

Chessie, Kathy and Leonard remained at the forefront, and Luca stood there watching. Cheering Nicky on. Hoping he really was enjoying himself.

"That looks like fun," said a familiar, deep voice from behind her.

Startled, yet pleased, Luca turned to see Mark there, looking at her with an unreadable but apparently caring expression. Rocky stood at his side.

"I agree," she said. "I think Nicky's going to miss it here, but I'm going to do my best to make sure he has all the fun he wants with other dogs wherever we end up."

"I'd like to talk to you about that," Mark said. Something changed in his expression. It looked more serious and yet…even more caring?

Or maybe her hopefulness was reading something into it. Maybe he was working up the nerve to say goodbye even sooner than she'd anticipated.

"Okay," she said as brightly as she could.

"Can we go to your apartment? I assume it'll be okay to leave Nicky for a while with the staffers here to do more playing and training and all."

"I'll make sure," Luca said, wondering what this was all about.

Yes, the staff members seemed delighted to spend more time with Nicky and even said they'd take him into the cafeteria for lunch soon.

She accompanied Mark down the shelter's center walkway toward the apartment building. There, with his dog, they walked up the steps to the floor where her apartment was, and went inside.

As soon as he closed the door behind them, Mark took her into his arms.

Their kiss was even more amazing than the ones they'd shared before, and those had been pretty amazing.

"Wow," she said when he finally stepped back. "That was fun but—"

"Come here." He led her into her living room before they sat on her sofa, facing one another. "I've got some things to share with you, and ask you." He continued before she could ask any questions. "When Rocky and I took our walk this morning, we went to the police station. I talked again to Sherm, told him that my working here undercover probably didn't make sense anymore, since too many people probably know, or at least suspect, that I'm a cop and I've been on an undercover assignment here."

"I wouldn't be surprised," Luca said. "Leonard was asking you before."

Mark nodded. "And my original undercover assignment didn't yield any results, so it might not have been necessary in the first place despite whatever rumors the authorities, and Scott, had been hearing. So I asked Sherm if I could return to the station, take on a different assignment for the Chance PD, maybe as an official K-9 cop with Rocky, as I had been before I came here."

"And?" she asked. She wondered if part of his reason was that he wouldn't want to stay at the shelter if she wasn't there.

Or was she hoping too much.

"And he said yes. So, like you, I'll soon be taking back my real name, which is Clark Martindale."

Luca laughed. "Hi, Clark."

"Hi, Cathleen. Now, here's my idea…" Mark reached over and took her hand into his firm, warm grip. His gaze looked…well, caring. More than caring. Loving?

Oh, yes, she was definitely hoping too much.

Or was she?

"The police department has several apartments for its officers to use when they're new to town or otherwise in need of someplace to stay, and Sherm says one is vacant now. What I'd like is for you and Nicky to move there with me. It's a bit too soon to say our being together will be permanent—but I'm really hoping that things will work out."

"Really?" Luca breathed. Wow. She hoped that too. Premature or not.

"While I was at the station, I did some online research about financial firms in the Chance area. There are quite a few, and when I checked I saw at least a couple are looking to hire new accountants, so I suspect you'll be able to find a job and not worry about whether I'd support the two of you—although I would. The cowboy in me wouldn't allow otherwise."

"That's so sweet," Luca said. She hurled herself forward into his arms. "And I love your idea. Yes, let's give it a try. I've got a feeling things will work out well that way."

She kissed him, and it turned into a long, wonderful, sexy kiss.

"Too bad I don't have any wine here," she whispered as this kiss ended. "I'd love to propose a toast to our future."

"Water will do," Mark said, nuzzling her neck. "Or just a promise to do a real toast when we head to town tomorrow. For now, here's a dry toast to us, and Nicky, and even Rocky. Let's have a wonderful, safe and loving future together."

"I'll drink to that," Luca said with a laugh and then kissed him again.

* * * * *

Don't miss the previous books in
Linda O. Johnston's Shelter of Secrets.
Look for:

Her Undercover Refuge
Guardian K-9 on Call

You'll find them wherever
Harlequin Romantic Suspense
books are sold!

#2223 COLTON'S BODY OF PROOF
The Coltons of New York • by Karen Whiddon

Officer Ellie Mathers just spotted her high school best friend... who's been missing for sixteen years. Reuniting with ex Liam Colton is the only way to solve the mystery. But is Ellie's biggest threat the flying bullets targeting her...or the sparks still flying between her and Liam?

#2224 OPERATION WITNESS PROTECTION
Cutter's Code • by Justine Davis

Twisted family secrets are exposed when Case McMillan saves a woman from an attack. But Terri Johnson's connection to the powerful Foxworth Foundation is only the beginning. She's now in a murderer's crosshairs, challenging *everything*, from Case's former job as a cop to his carefully guarded heart.

#2225 COLD CASE SHERIFF
Sierra's Web • by Tara Taylor Quinn

Aimee Barker has had nightmares since her parents' murder. Now she's being shot at! Sheriff Jackson Redmond vows to protect the vulnerable beauty and help her solve the cold case. But can he offer the loving home she craves once his connection to the suspect is revealed?

#2226 HER K-9 PROTECTOR
Big Sky Justice • by Kimberly Van Meter

Single mom Kenna Griffin is running from a dangerous ex. But her fresh start is complicated by K-9 cop Lucas Merritt...and her deepening feelings for him. She's scared to trust him with her love and her dark secrets. Keeping them hidden could get them both killed...

HRSCNM0223

HARLEQUIN
PLUS

Try the best multimedia subscription service for romance readers like you!

Read, Watch and Play.

Experience the easiest way to get the romance content you crave.

Start your **FREE TRIAL** at
www.harlequinplus.com/freetrial.